SAWYER'S RUN

A (mostly) fictional Appalachian
Trail adventure

Lee Lovelace

Copyright © 2021 Lee Lovelace

All rights reserved

The characters and events portrayed in this book are fictitious. Except where permission has been granted to use real names, any similarity to real persons, living or dead, is coincidental and not intended by the author.

No part of this book may be reproduced, or stored in a retrieval system, or transmitted in any form or by any means, electronic, mechanical, photocopying, recording, or otherwise, without express written permission of the publisher.

Cover design by: Gabe Burkhardt
Printed in the United States of America

Dedicated to my Golden Retriever Sawyer, and my wife, without her support I could have never written this book.

Also, I guess I dedicate it a little bit to the real life ranger that inspired this tale. But only a little bit.

A special dedication to my good friend, Gabe Burkhardt. He drew the sketch for the cover art to this book. Gabe passed away on a hike in 2020. He touched so many people's life and is missed by many. Keep on trekking, Gabe!

It's a dangerous business, Frodo, going out your door. You step onto the road, and if you don't keep your feet, there's no telling where you might be swept off to.

J.R.R. TOLKIEN

CONTENTS

Title Page

Copyright

Dedication

Dedication

Epigraph

MAP OF THE APPALACHIAN TRAIL

MAP OF SHENANDOAH NATIONAL PARK

CHAPTER ONE   1

CHAPTER TWO   6

CHAPTER THREE   37

CHAPTER FOUR   43

CHAPTER FIVE   48

CHAPTER SIX   53

CHAPTER SEVEN   59

CHAPTER EIGHT   81

CHAPTER NINE   100

CHAPTER TEN   107

CHAPTER ELEVEN   123

CHAPTER TWELVE   133

CHAPTER THIRTEEN   143

CHAPTER FOURTEEN   144

Acknowledgement	149
About The Author	151
Review	153

MAP OF THE APPALACHIAN TRAIL

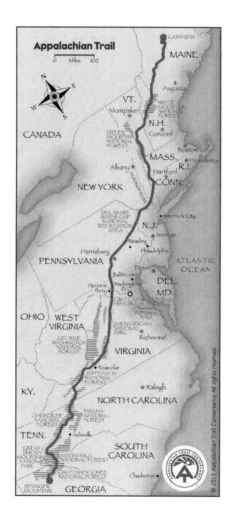

MAP OF SHENANDOAH NATIONAL PARK

CHAPTER ONE

Damascus

Dad

I was standing at the beginning of an adventure of a lifetime. Right beside me, linked through an elastic leash clipped to my belt, was Sawyer, my golden retriever. We were both looking at a wooden sign that read:

APPALACHIAN TRAIL
WELCOME
DAMASCUS VA

We were going to spend the better part of the next three months hiking the Appalachian Trail through our home state of Virginia and beyond. It *was* going to be the adventure of a lifetime. Just not in the way we thought it would be. That's up the trail a ways though.

This was day one of the hike, and my wife had just dropped us off here at the Damascus Town Park where the famous sign marks the entrance of the trail into the town. I say it's famous, but only to hikers and people familiar with the trail. The Appalachian Trail is roughly 2200 miles of scenic trail that stretches from Springer Mountain in Georgia to the summit of Katahdin in Maine. Sawyer and I were going to hike the 555 miles from Damascus, Virginia to Harpers Ferry, West Virginia. Let me rephrase that. We were going to *attempt* to hike those

555 miles. Neither one of us were new to hiking or backpacking. We'd done countless day hikes and many overnight hikes, but the longest we'd ever been out on a trail was two days. I wanted to push ourselves and see if we were up to a multi-day hiking trip. I don't know about Sawyer, but I had nervous butterflies in my stomach thinking about it. There was also excitement passing through my entire body like I was more alive than ever. That feeling far outweighed any nervous ones, and I was ready to get to it.

This was a whole new kind of hike and would test our mettle in the backcountry. Every year there were people called thru-hikers that walked the whole trail from Georgia to Maine (north-bounders or NOBO's), or from Maine to Georgia (south-bounders or SOBO's.) I would have loved us to do this challenge, but it takes five to six months to accomplish. Taking off three months was difficult enough. Sawyer and I were section hiking, just doing a portion of the trail. Actually, we were doing a long section. The Appalachian Trail goes through fourteen states, and Virginia was home to more miles of the trail than any other state. In the hiking community there was a name for that kind of section hiking—it's called a LASH. Long Ass Section Hike. We were LASHers.

My wife dropped us off, but we didn't linger in our goodbyes. We had stayed at the Dragonfly Inn Bed & Breakfast the night before and had done all the proper goodbyes then. It was going to be a long time spent apart, but we had made plans for her to meet us at least once during the hike so we wouldn't be apart for the whole three months.

"You ready to do this thing?" I asked Sawyer. He looked back at me and I could swear he winked. "Sometimes I think you know exactly what I'm saying, don't you boy?"

Sawyer

SAWYER'S RUN

Yes, I'm ready to do this thing and I do, for the most part, know what you're saying. I'm just not equipped to communicate that to you. It's not the first time that Dad has said that to me, and it's not the first time that I've had the same thought. I was definitely ready to do this thing, though. I loved hiking with Dad. I loved being outside and smelling all the unfamiliar scents and seeing all the new places. I'm not fond of the heat, with this furry coat of mine acting as a winter parka all the time. It's not that bad today, so I am cool with it. Cool. See what I did there? Dogs can have a sense of humor too. It's only entertaining to me, though, because of the whole not equipped to communicate thing.

The one thing I didn't like was my damn backpack that Dad strapped to me when we hike. It's just a little thing that has my water and snacks in it but it's annoying and makes me hot. I looked up at Dad and gave him a wink, but then I shook my back a little to show him I'm not amused with the pack. Even if it has a clever little name, Outward Hound, I don't want it. Why can't Dad just carry it in that big pack? Oh well, I'll tough it out for now and maybe throw a little tantrum later. Don't want to spoil the beginning of this adventure, do I?

Dad

We began our hike. The trail goes through the middle of the town of Damascus for a few miles. For now, we weren't in the woods. Damascus was nicknamed Trail Town, USA. It's the intersection of eight local, state, and national trails, the Appalachian Trail being the most famous, and commonly just called the AT by locals and hikers. It's a small town, but every year in late May they host a Trail Days festival that brings in several thousand hikers and outdoor enthusiasts. We've never been, and it sounded interesting, but it was early May when we began our hike so we would be long gone by then.

Sawyer and I walked the streets and sidewalks through town.

Sawyer did great walking by my side. That would probably change once we got in the woods. He loved to trudge ahead in the mornings and always got out in front of me, slightly tugging on the leash to tell me to hurry up. For now though, he was sticking close by until he saw a cat sitting on a porch of a nearby house and wanted to go investigate it.

"No Sawyer! Leave the cat alone." That and two tugs on the leash and he fell back in line.

We continued on for the next hour, walking past the Mt. Rogers Outfitters store with a beautiful mural of the mountainside landscape painted on the exterior of one wall. We also passed other interesting sights such as a bicycle rental place called the Shuttle Shack, another outfitter called Sun Dogs, and a place named Crazy Larry's Hostel. A hostel was a place that tired hikers could get off the trail and stay for a night or two. I'd read accounts from hiker blogs on stays in hostels. It was mostly like a communal living arrangement. It sounded like most hikers had positive experiences staying in them. I had always been curious about hostels but the whole communal thing kind of made me nervous. I wasn't sure if we would stay in one on this trip, but as we were only an hour into the hike, it was a moot point.

The whole small town scene was very quaint and felt homey. I wondered how it was to live here and how the town handled the mass influx of hikers during Trail Days.

Sawyer

Dad led me through the town. I could see him looking around at things, but for me it was kind of boring, except for the little excitement with that fuzz ball. That cat gave me the stink eye and I had intended to close it for him, but Dad wasn't going to have any of that. Oh well.

I was glad when we left the town behind and walked along

the road with trees on both sides and a small creek on our right. The smell of the vegetation and the sound of the gently babbling water was more to my liking. It was time to get to proper hiking!

CHAPTER TWO

Northbound

Dad

We left the town and turned off the highway north where the trail entered the woods. It was a thousand foot climb to the top of the first mountain and time to test ourselves. Sawyer got out front and started straining on the leash. I tried to keep up, and did, for the most part, until the grade got steeper. This didn't seem to bother Sawyer, and I had to rein him in some so I could keep pace. I was leaning heavily on my walking stick to help me climb the grade. I had a pair of lightweight trekking poles that did a better job at helping distribute the weight. They worked great when I was hiking alone, but they got caught up in the hiking leash when Sawyer was with me. For this reason, I brought my walking stick instead. Several years ago my, now grown, sons gave me the walking stick as a birthday present because they knew how much I liked to hike. It's a hefty stick that came up to my shoulders with a leather strap about a quarter length from the top. At the bottom was a rubber tip that kept it from scraping along the rock or tearing up the dirt. As long as I kept it in the hand on the opposite side of where the hiking leash was attached, it wouldn't get caught up. I also liked using the stick because it reminded me of when my sons would go on hikes with me. A number of years earlier, we spent a week camping in the Shenandoah National Park. We went on several day hikes from our base camp and had a great time. Sawyer spent that trip with us also. In the years to follow, the boys became busy making their own adult lives and didn't have the time to hang out in the woods with the old man. Sawyer was still here though, and that was just fine.

A little while later, Sawyer and I made it to the top and had a spectacular view of the valley below. We could see tree covered mountains for miles, all dotted every now and then with houses and farms. I would have loved to take up residence at anyone of them. We could also see the White Top Laurel River, that the Virginia Creeper trail followed, wind its way through the mountainsides. The blue waters flowed smoothly at some points and formed white frothed turbulent rapids at others. The AT and the Virginia Creeper trails ran close together for the next thirty miles and sometimes merged. We chose this picturesque spot to have lunch. I dropped my pack, then unbuckled and pulled Sawyer's pack off. He looked happier. I knew he hated that thing, but I couldn't carry everything. My pack weighed thirty-five pounds without water. Lunch for me consisted of slices of summer sausage with cheddar cheese rolled in a soft tortilla shell. Sawyer got dry food and a few snacks from his pack. We both drank water from our bottles. I was carrying two one liter Smart Water bottles with a filter screwed to the one I was actively drinking from. Sawyer carried two sixteen-ounce bottles filled with filtered water. We were both down to one bottle from drinking on the ascent and what we had downed during lunch. I consulted the Guthook AT Guide application on my phone and saw the next water source was about two miles away. We would have to refill there. Guthook's was a handy mapping app for the AT. It worked with preloaded maps and a GPS signal. You didn't have to have cell service to use it, so it cut down on battery drain.

Sawyer

When we finally entered the woods I opened it up a bit and got out in front of Dad. I got as far as I could and felt the leash reign me in. Dad pulled back and told me to slow down. *Damn Dad! Why don't you just let me off this thing so I can roam free?* He actually had let me off once on a day hike and I had screwed it up. I didn't mean to take off, I just couldn't help myself. I was so happy to be off leash I ran far ahead up the trail, exploring all the wonderful things. When I finally looked back I realized I was alone. Oops. I had slinked back up the trail to find Dad out of breath, sitting on a log. He hooked me back up, gave me a ration of shit, and I've never been off leash again on the trail. Oh well, I could still have fun on leash too.

We climbed up a steep hill and while it looked like I had no problem; it was tiring. But again, I have four legs and Dad only has two, ha! When we got to the top, we took a break and had some lunch. Dad attached me to the long leash and tied it around the base of a tree. The long leash was awesome because I could wander around a lot farther. Only thing was I got it caught up and wound around things sometimes. You'd think as smart as I was this wouldn't happen, but I lost track of where the leash was when I was distracted by all the different scents and wonderful views. Dad also took that damn pack off my back, which made me immediately happy. I knew it was only temporary, but I was glad to be free of that thing for a bit.

Dad stuffed his face with people food and gave me some of my dry kibble and a few dog snacks. I'd much rather have some wet food but I know he had that saved for dinner tonight. After we ate and did some business (which Dad had to bury because it was close to the trail) we admired the view for a little longer, and then started gearing up. Dad made the mistake of trying to put my pack on while I was on the long leash. It was time for a little demonstration on how much I hated that pack. I shrugged him off and ran to the length of the leash. When he tried to chase me down, I ran the opposite way. I did this twice before he wound up the leash and hauled me in. He got the pack strapped back on me, but I had one more show of disgust. I flopped over on my back and squirmed around on the ground, making my thoughts of dissatisfaction known. Dad just watched for a few seconds and then I gave in and stood up ready to resume the hike.

Dad

We spent the rest of the afternoon, surprisingly enough, hiking. We descended another thousand feet to the valley floor. Some people might think going down was a lot easier than going up. Some people would be wrong, at least for me. Going down just presented different difficulties than going up.

"What do I always say Sawyer?" He looked up at me to signal he knew what I was about to say. "Up hurts my heart. Down hurts my knees. Level is just fine with me. Of course, it wouldn't be hiking in the mountains if it was always level, would it be boy?" I could have sworn I saw Sawyer shake his head at me. If he could talk, he would tell me to get new material. I gave him a wink and scratched his head and ears. The eyes in his head rolled back. He loved a good head and ears scratch.

I had problems with my knees aching on descents. A couple of years ago, my wife bought me some knee supports that secured with Velcro straps. They helped immensely and I'd been wearing them on hikes ever since. After refilling our water at a stream, we began another 1200 foot climb. I was running out of steam and this one took some time. I wasn't the only one that was running out of steam. True to form, Sawyer wasn't pulling on the leash anymore. Now he was lagging, and I had to tug the leash from time to time to keep him on pace. We took more frequent breaks on this ascent. I started encouraging myself in my head. *Just make it to that tree. That's all you have to do.* Then I would get to the tree and tell myself *just to that rock that looks like a huge pile of bear poop.* I would plant my walking stick, dig in, and haul my ass up there. In this manner we eventually made it to the top where things leveled out a bit. Thank God!

LEE LOVELACE

Speaking of bears, the Appalachian Trail was home to a significant number of American Black Bear. We hadn't seen any today, but I expected we would before the trip was over. There is a high concentration of black bears in the Shenandoah National Park we would hike through toward the end of the trip. Sawyer and I both had seen a few black bears on previous hikes, but our views had been of their butts as they ran away. Most bears don't want to have anything to do with humans, or canines, and as long as you don't get between a mother and her cub, they'll take off when you encounter them, most of the time. We had never had a close up encounter with a bear and we weren't planning one soon.

We came to a side trail that ran about 0.25 miles to the Saunders Shelter, where we would hang our hats for the night. I took the turn to head down the side trail and Sawyer balked a bit, trying to continue up the AT. Sawyer had a keen sense of navigation. He often instinctively knew the right way to go and had gotten me "unlost" a few times.

"I know you're following the white blazes boy, but we are done for today and the shelter is this way."

They mark the path of the AT with a 2" x 6" white stripe of paint on trees (sometimes rocks), called a blaze. The tree we were looking at had two white blazes side by side on it. Two blazes meant there was an intersection on the trail, like the side trail to the shelter. Two white blazes could also indicate a change in direction of the trail and were usually painted with one slightly higher than the other. They painted side trails with blue-blazes and, I could see another tree down the side trail with the distinctive blue paint. The explanation seemed to satisfy Sawyer because when I started down the blue-blaze trail again, he followed.

Sawyer

Get new material, Dad! You know how many times I've heard

him say that? Oh well, I'd rather be out here listening to Dad-isms and getting good head and ear scratches than back home cooped up in the house or the fenced-in backyard. I gave him a big smile, which he and Mom always called my *Colebrook Smile*. Colebrook Farms was where I was born and all my sisters, brother, and cousins evidently had similar smiles. At least that's what they claimed from looking at pictures on something called Facebook. I'd heard Mom talk about a group she ran that kept track of Colebrook dogs.

Man, this climb was a bitch. I was now letting Dad take the lead. He thinks I'm too tired to be out front, but I just thought I'd let him get his turn. Yeah, that's what I was doing. Did I already tell you this climb was a bitch? OK, I was happy to stop and rest every time Dad did.

At the top, I could see that Dad was relieved to be walking level again. So was I. We stopped for a rest and Dad pulled out my collapsible water dish. He filled it up with a bottle from my pack and I lapped it up. I was hoping this would be a "packs off" break, but he didn't take mine or his off, damn it. After that break, we continued up the trail before Dad tried to go the wrong way. Here we go again. I don't know how many times I've course corrected this dude when we were hiking. I pulled a little on the leash, indicating he was going the wrong way, but he stopped me and said something about blazes. I didn't really know what he was talking about. All I knew was that the other way was the big trail. Then he said something about being done for the day and we were going to a shelter. Now *that* I understood, and it sounded fine with me! I ceased my protest and followed him down the other trail.

Dad

We reached Saunders shelter and were the only ones there. It was just after 5:00 PM and we had hiked about ten miles. I wondered if we'd be the only ones here tonight. The AT had shelters built all along its length. They were often three-sided open shelters that you could throw a sleeping bag in and stay somewhat out of the elements. I didn't like staying in the shelters for a few reasons. One, I had Sawyer and if the shelter was full, it was hard to keep him out of other people's way. Two, mice knew to hang out at the shelters to get food and I have known them to crawl across a hiker's face in the middle of the night. Not a fan. Three, I snored, not just like a freight train, but a freight train that derailed and crashed into the middle of a fireworks factory. It did not endear me to other hikers. We had stayed overnight in a few shelters when we were the only ones there and it was raining, but our usual abode was a tent. Most shelters had spaces around to set up a tent, and this one was no exception.

After doffing our packs, I grabbed the shelter log and sat down at the picnic table in front for a bit of rest. I hooked Sawyer to his 20-foot long leash and tied it off to the table. After a few cursory investigative wanderings, he curled up under the table to take a nap. I rested for about 15 minutes while I read the log. There was a log in the form of a spiral notebook in each shelter for hikers to write in. It served as a communication system up and down the trail. Hikers could leave notes for others they knew or for the general hiking community. Some hikers used the logs to showcase their writing or artistic talents and could be highly entertaining. One particular entry that was written in the log a few weeks ago hit me in the feels.

Be loyal. Drink good beer. Love all who love and support you. Give no shit. Take no shit. Stand up for someone weak. Give back. Don't steal. Don't lie. Don't cheat. Protect something til death. Bang hard. Love harder...Take care of your people...Be part of something bigger than yourself. Learn how to listen to shoot. Listen to good music often. Eat well. Love all animals. Crush anyone who harms women, the disabled, or children. Be the example. Live it.

All great advice and made me really happy to be out there. My own entry was not as inspiring.

Here we began our LASH. See you in Harpers Ferry! We hope.

Once I was done contributing that work of art, I got busy. There were chores to be done when you got to camp. I pulled our REI Passage two-man tent (more accurately, one man/one dog) from my pack and set it up in a level spot several yards away from the shelter. According to the weather report, it wasn't supposed to rain tonight but I set up the rain fly anyway. I'd been burned before by an erroneous weather report that necessitated a 2 AM emergency fly installation.

With that done, I pulled off my hiking shoes and replaced them with my camp shoes. My camp shoes were a pair of Crocs. Not the most stylish of footwear but in the backcountry they were perfect for knocking around in camp, and they were light so they didn't add too much weight to my pack. I checked on Sawyer, who was still sleeping under the table, and then headed to a piped stream about 100 yards from the back of the shelter. There I filtered and refilled all our water bottles. Getting water wasn't as easy as just scooping it from a stream. The water could contain parasites like Giardia, which will make a hiker sick. Symptoms can range from diarrhea (bad enough on the trail) to debilitating stomach cramps, nausea and weakness. In order to prevent this, I used a Sawyer water filter to strain out any parasites or dirt from the water. No, it's not Sawyer's water filter. The company that made one of the best filters was named Sawyer. That I used a Sawyer filter to filter water for a dog named Sawyer was just an interesting coincidence.

The filter came with water bags that you used to scoop water from a stream or other source. The inlet side of the filter screwed to the top of the bag and you squeezed it to force the dirty water through the filter screens inside, and produce clean water at the other end. Then you filled up your water bottles with this clean water. Another way to filter water was to use a plastic water bottle (Smart Water bottles were sturdy and worked well) to collect water, and then screw the filter directly to the top of the bottle. In this configuration, I could drink directly from the filter, and fill up Sawyer's smaller bottles or water bowl. This is the method I chose to use most often as it seemed to be a little less work for me and I didn't have to carry water bags.

Now was the time to do my least favorite task. Hanging the bear bag. All our food except for snacks I kept in my hip belt pockets for eating along the trail, were in a waterproof sack, commonly known as a bear bag. Its purpose was to keep the woodland creatures, not just bears, from raiding our food. I took out the food we were going to be eating for dinner and then began this procedure. I found a rock about the size of my hand and put it in a little sack that had para-cord attached to it. The idea is to hang your bear bag in a tree at least 200 feet away from your tent or the shelter. You wanted to get it about 15 feet off the ground and at least 5 feet away from the trunk of the tree. At this point things usually go awry. I located a good candidate tree limb, swung my rock bag around in a circle a few times to build up momentum, and then released it. It missed by a mile and it fell to the ground. I picked it up and tried again. The bag got caught up in the smaller branches further along the limb and stuck. I heaved down on the cord but the bag would not come loose. Standing directly under the bag I got a good grip on the cord and put all my weight (not inconsequential) on it. The tree limb bent and just when I thought it wasn't going to release the payload, it did, straight down! The rock bag took a direct trajectory to my head, knocking me senseless! I staggered back a few steps and then hit the ground, where I sat there rubbing my noggin. When I could think straight again, I glanced around to see if anyone had come to the shelter while I was attempting this pathetic excuse for a bear bag hang. Luckily no one had, and even Sawyer was still asleep. Dignity still (somewhat) intact, I tried again. It took me five more tries but I finally got it up and over the limb without further injuring myself.

I removed the rock bag and tied a carabiner to the end of the cord. I then hooked the carabiner to a loop on my bear bag. I slipped the other end of the cord that was hanging across the limb into the carabiner so I could now haul down on it and the bag would rise. I pulled the bag until it was almost to the tree limb. Reaching above my head I tied a loop knot and stuck a small stick that I had found on the ground through the loop and cinched it tight. I let up on my grip on the cord and the weight of the bag caused it to come down, but the stick rose up and when it reached the carabiner it held fast, keeping the bag hanging about two feet below the limb. The beauty was that with this type of hang, if a bear or other creature tried to grab the cord, all it would do was raise the bag higher and it would protect the food. If I wanted to get anything else out of or put into the bag, I just had to slide the cord down until I could reach the stick and remove it from the loop knot, lowering the bag all the way to the ground.

Now that most of the chores were done, it was time to sit back and enjoy one of the best parts of the night, eating! I pulled my lightweight Jet Boil camping stove out of my pack and set it up on the table. I filled the integrated pot with water and lit the stove. Upon hearing this commotion, Sawyer awoke from his nap and laid his head upon the table bench, watching the preparations.

"Oh, awake now that all the chores are done and it's time to eat, huh?" I teased him. He just continued to stare, wondering when I would dish up his dinner.

I did just that while waiting for my water to come to a boil. He got a mixture of dry dog food and a wet dog food pack, which he lapped up greedily even before my water had come to a boil. Now it was my turn. I slid over my freeze-dried Mountain House meal. These were about the best freeze dried meals you could have on the trail. They were expensive, so I wouldn't be having one every night, but I had earmarked one for the first night. Tonight's selection was Italian Style Pepper Steak, one of my personal favorites. I ripped the top off of the bag and withdrew the desiccant freshness pack. I took the pot from my stove and poured in the boiling water. Sealing up the bag, I let it sit for ten minutes to cook.

During this time, I cleaned out Sawyer's bowl and filled it with fresh water. When the ten minutes was up I opened up the bag, took out my Sea to Summit metal spork, and got busy. It was delicious. I looked at Sawyer and said, "You were such a good dog today, I'm going to give you a treat." I gave him the last two spoonful's of my dinner, which he graciously accepted. With that done, I gathered up all the trash and stuffed it in a big zip lock bag that I had brought for just that purpose. I was a firm believer in the *Leave No Trace* policy. If you pack it in, you pack it out. Just as I had finished sealing up the trash, Sawyer stood and walked several feet toward the trail, cocking his head inquisitively.

A moment later, two male hikers, who appeared to be in their 20s, came from around the bend and headed in our direction. They stopped when they saw Sawyer advance to the length of his leash.

"No worries!" I shouted to them. "He's a big teddy bear. You only have to be worried about being licked to death."

They laughed and came over to the table, pausing briefly to give Sawyer a few pats. They had all the looks of thru-hikers. By this I meant they were dirty, unshaved, and carrying big backpacks that had any number of items hanging from them, such as water bottles, rolled up sleeping bags, and camp shoes. Oh yeah, they stunk too! Showers were hard to come by on the trail. I only knew they stunk because it was our first day of the hike. I would find out later as I stank myself, I couldn't smell it on other hikers. Well, most other hikers. There were a select few that exhibited an odor on another level that would always be identifiable. To be sure, I asked if they were thru-hikers and they acknowledged they were. "What are your trail names?" I inquired.

The taller of the two said, "I'm Early Bird."

The shorter said, "Worm."

Trail names are nicknames that thru-hikers or LASHers take

on while they are hiking the trail. Typically, these names are bestowed upon them by fellow hikers, and they usually convey something about that hiker. Often it's the only name a hiker was known by in the community. I have even known dogs to have trail names. Sawyer and I didn't have trail names because we had never been out on the trail long enough to get one. I was wondering if we might get them during this three month hike.

"I know you've been asked a thousand times," I said to them. "But I have to know how you got them." This was almost always the way conversations first started between hikers meeting on the trail.

Worm relayed the story of their monikers. "Early Bird over there likes to get up early to start hiking, so no mystery there. Thing is, I get up just as early and usually beat him out of camp by 30 minutes or so. But he's fast and usually overtakes me in no time. So I became the "worm" that the early bird gets."

I chuckled at this. "Clever!" I told them.

Early Bird and Worm were going to stay in the shelter, so they set about doing their camp chores and had some dinner. I did some necessaries, like brushing my teeth and a trip to the privy I'm not sure you would want more details about. I am going to give you some, though. Having a privy, which is pretty much a hole in the ground covered by a shack, was a luxury. Otherwise, you dig a hole in the woods (called a cat hole) and hope your aim is as good as Tom Brady completing a touchdown pass. I have been known to "throw" the ball out of bounds on occasion, which makes quite the mess. I also took Sawyer out to do his business. I wasn't digging a cat hole (or dog hole) for him though. He wouldn't use the privy and the way I figured it, he was an animal so he could go in the woods. Some people don't think this is following the no trace policy but I didn't care. It wasn't like I was letting him take a dump right in the middle of the trail or camping spot.

Once those activities were completed, I lowered the bear bag and stuffed it with the trash and anything else that had a scent. I didn't want any ursine encounters during the night looking for a pic-a-nic basket in my tent. With the bag safely hoisted back in the sky, Sawyer and I sat back down on logs around the fire ring.

There were too many trees around the shelter to see the sunset, but it was still a serene scene as the light slowly ran away and darkness approached. Before it was fully dark, Early Bird built a fire and we sat around chatting. Sawyer looked like he was paying attention to the conversation as he laid near the log at my feet. The chat was mostly the typical hiker fair. Where we were from, how many miles we averaged a day (we just got started so it was low compared to theirs), and gear talk. I had a good time talking to these guys who seemed to be friendly, even if they were younger than me. Aside from the occasional asshole, most everyone I had met while hiking was a good person. Age could play a part when it came to some activities, but for the most part everyone identified with being in the same community and wanted to watch out for each other.

After about an hour of chatting, we noticed it was around 7:30 and we prepared to hit the sack. If you are a non-hiker you probably think that's pretty early but it really isn't. On the trail in the backcountry, there was a time commonly referred to as *Hiker's Midnight*. It's usually around 8 PM and for hikers that have been climbing mountains all day, it's the time when the body says *OK buddy, time to get some rest*. It's pretty much universally agreed upon in the hiking community, that even if you aren't going to bed, it's time to keep the noise down for those that are.

I said goodnight to Early Bird and Worm, and Sawyer and I headed for the tent. Sometimes I have to cajole Sawyer into the tent, but not tonight. He barely let me get the zipper open before he pushed his way in and laid down in his spot near the far side at the foot of my sleeping bag. I pulled in my pack, changed into my sleeping clothes, and snuggled into the bag. I laid there for a few minutes listening to all the woodland noises and a wide smile crept on my face. Our first day on this hiking trip was complete.

Sawyer

Once we were at the shelter site Dad took off my pack (done with that damnable thing for today) and switched me to my long leash. This gave me plenty of length to check things out. I walked around smelling everything. There were some human scents, but there were some creature ones too. Some were ones I knew, like squirrels and birds. Other ones I was not familiar with but I cataloged them in case I ever got to meet their owners. When I had smelt everything I could, I went and got under the table so I could catch some shade. I knew what was coming next and I would not be a part of it. Yup, Dad set about doing all the chores. I watched for a moment, and then caught myself a little shuteye. A little while later I woke to the sound of Dad doing his cowboy thing. I cracked open one eye just enough to see him trying to throw the rope over a tree limb. He was failing miserably. I had been witness to this before and I know it embarrassed him when someone saw, so I pretended to still be asleep. I felt sorry for him and would have given him a hand but, you know, no opposable thumbs, so not much I could do. I saw him finally get it done and I slipped back into sleep knowing dinner would come after chores.

I awoke later to see Dad was getting dinner together, which was my cue to get my butt up. Well, I actually barely moved my butt just enough so I could lay my head on the table bench and watch.

"Oh, awake now that all the chores are done and it's time to eat, huh?" Dad said to me.

Well, yeah, duh. I haz cheeseburger?

It was wishful thinking though. Dad mixed up some dry food with the wet and put it in my bowl. Good enough. I was starving! I wolfed it down. He also gave me a couple of bites from what he was eating and that rounded out the meal.

What was that noise? I could hear somebody coming up the

trail. *Hey Dad, we got visitors.* He hadn't even heard them yet. It was my job to investigate the situation. I walked over to the trail and cocked my head. Then I saw two guys come around the bend and head our way. I have a sixth sense for humans. I can usually tell if they are good or bad. These guys were giving off a good vibe, so I wagged my tail. They stopped when they caught sight of me, and I heard Dad say something about me being a teddy bear. Ugh, I really wish he wouldn't say that to people. Just because I didn't rip people apart didn't mean I couldn't. I just chose not to unless the situation called for it. Fortunately, it had never called for it in my entire life. Teddy bear my furry ass. Let me get sight of an uppity cat and I would show you how much of a teddy bear I am not.

We sat around the fire while Dad chatted with the new guys. I half listened but was more interested in the head scratches I was getting from Dad as I laid near him and the log he was sitting on. While we did that, Dad broke out some lotion and rubbed it on my paws. I wasn't too thrilled with having my paws messed with, but I noticed later on that they were not as sore as they had been when we got to camp. That Dad person was a pretty cool dude.

A little while later the party broke up, they put the fire out, and we went about doing our last bit of business by the light of that thing on Dad's head. I think he called it a headlamp. Once our business was done we headed toward the tent. Sometimes when we overnight hike I act a little hesitant before going in the tent. I actually liked being in the tent, but it just felt like something a dog should do, so I would balk for a few seconds. But tonight I was dog tired (see what I did there?) despite the earlier nap I had, and couldn't wait to get in and lay down. Once I got in my spot and Dad was all tucked in, I could rest for the night.

Dad

The next morning I poked my head out of the tent around 6:30. Early Bird and Worm were true to their trail names. They were already gone. I didn't even hear them pack up. Except for a 3 AM trip out for both Sawyer and me to relieve ourselves, I had slept soundly all night.

We had a quick breakfast and packed up. My muscles were sore from the previous day's exertions, but I figured I'd get used to it soon enough. As soon as we had packed everything up, we headed back down the blue-blaze trail to the intersection with the AT.

I stopped, looked at Sawyer, and asked, "Which way buddy?" Not that I didn't know. I just wanted to see what he'd do. He didn't even hesitate and turned left, heading north on the trail and pulling me behind on the leash. Sometimes I wondered who had who on the leash.

So up the trail we went and in the next few days things started to become routine. We hiked, we took a break, we hiked some more, we found a good spot for lunch (usually with a good view and somewhere flat to sit), we hiked some more, we took another break, we hiked some more, and then we found a spot to camp for the night. Sometimes we camped at a shelter and sometimes we camped at a good flat spot in the woods.

At one point we crossed into Grayson Highlands State Park. While we were passing over one of the balds (mountaintops with no trees) we saw a group of wild ponies hanging around. I saw a few hikers ahead of us offer them some treats, but when the ponies started to approach us, Sawyer barked at them. They stopped in their tracks, and when he barked again, they reversed course and gave us a wide berth. "Thanks a lot, Sawyer! I wanted to pet them." He just looked at me with a proud expression on his face. Guess he figured he'd done his job protecting us from those dangerous equines.

Four days into the hike we had to resupply because we were only carrying that many days' worth of food, with a little extra in case of emergencies. To carry more than that was just too heavy. Near the Partnership Shelter, which was a huge shelter that accommodated about twenty people, was the Mt. Rogers Outdoor Center. Here you could call a shuttle to take you into the town of Marion. I thought I might have a problem with them letting Sawyer on it, but the driver didn't even look twice.

In town, we walked to Walmart and resupplied. Again, no problem with taking a dog inside. We walked across the street to a McDonald's and pigged out on some "real" food. Micky D's wasn't too keen on a dog inside, and I could understand that. I tied Sawyer's hiking leash to a parking post outside, but where I could see him through the window, and went in and got our food. We ate at a table outside which the people inside were surely thankful for since I hadn't had a shower in four days. I wolfed down two Big Macs and Sawyer had no problem finishing off a 20 piece chicken McNuggets. I guess our hiker hunger was kicking in. Had to replace those calories we were burning on the mountains.

We caught the shuttle back to the trail and returned to the Partnership Shelter. I had planned to stay there for the night but I discovered there was no tenting allowed. I briefly considered staying in the shelter, but because it was so close to a trailhead, the place was packed. I decided to hike a few miles up to a tent spot marked on my Guthook app instead. I took advantage of one thing at this shelter before we left. They had a solar shower here! I got in and cleaned my nasty body. I tried to do the same for Sawyer but all I managed to do was get him wet and when he got out, he went and rolled in the dirt. This caused quite a bit of laughter from other hikers at the shelter and as frustrated as I was with the fur face, I couldn't help but laugh too.

A few days later we came out of the woods at some nondescript road crossing and saw people congregated around a folding table and a portable BBQ grill. Yes! This was our first encounter with Trail Magic. Trail Magic happened when people, out of the goodness of their hearts, came out to spots like this and fed hikers. Trail Magic can also come in the form of rides into town and even places to stay for the night. Often the magic comes from former thru or section hikers. Sometimes it comes from people that like to help out and are not hikers themselves. Sawyer, my wife, and I had provided Trail Magic a few times where the AT runs close to cabins where we vacationed, a little further north in Virginia. This magic did wonders for my spirit and helped rejuvenate my energy level. This event was being put on by a former thru-hiker named Stronghold.

"Thank you very much for doing this," I told him as I was grabbing a burger from a foil pan next to the grill he was manning.

"No prob, man. I get more out of this than you do."

"I know how you feel. I've done trail magic before and I say the same thing. First time I've been on this side of it though."

"Cool! Are you thru-hiking?"

"No, just a LASH through Virginia to Harpers Ferry."

"That's still a long haul."

"Yeah it is. I wish it could be longer. It's hard work but it is good for my soul. Makes me put things in perspective."

"I know what you mean. I'm an Army Vet. I saw some action in the Middle East. When I got out I just had a hard time letting it go. I started hiking and found it helped, so I did the big one, a thru-hike on the AT. My life hasn't been the same since. So I came back to pay forward some of the magic that I received."

"That is awesome man! I'm glad to hear it."

Sawyer and I downed some burgers and dogs and had a great time talking to all the other hikers there. Sometimes these Trail Magic events can be dangerous, making it easy to get sucked into the vortex and spend way too much time there when we should make miles. However, there is a saying that rings true with me. *It's all about the smiles, not the miles.* But eventually we pried our smiling faces away and continued hiking.

Sawyer

The next morning when we were all packed and hiking again,

we stopped at the trail intersection. Dad asked me which way we were going. *Are you kidding me, Dad? At least give me something challenging.* I turned left leading us in the correct direction and increased my pace a bit to tug him along.

The days stretched out as we hiked, ate, and camped. It was a great time. Sure, I got tired sometimes, but we always took well timed breaks to catch our breath. One day, we were hiking over a treeless mountain top and I saw these furry creatures milling about. I think they were called horses. I know I've seen them on TV and I've even seen them in real life once at Colonial Williamsburg. There, they had been pulling wagons. Here, they were free to roam about at will. The horses noticed us and started coming our way. Oh no, not on my watch! I had to protect Dad! I barked and bared my teeth at them and they turned tail and ran. I looked at Dad and smiled, expecting praise. He didn't seem to be all that grateful. I just saved his ass from some ferocious animals and I didn't even get a thankful head scratch? Sheesh.

Another day, I got to ride in a bus to a town. We went to a store and Dad got some more food for us to take on the trail. Then we got to go to McDonalds where I got to eat a bunch of chimkin nuggets! Once we were back at the trail, Dad herded me into this little shack and poured water all over me! *What the hell, Dad?* I wasn't having none of that and escaped his grasp. I needed to dry off but nobody was offering a towel so I did the next best thing. I rolled around in the dirt. This did not go over so well with Dad but all the other hikers started laughing and I admit, I enjoyed the attention.

Dad

One day we stopped at the Wapiti Shelter to eat lunch. This was an infamous spot on the trail. A murder occurred in this area. It was actually at the site of the original Wapiti Shelter, which was torn down but not too far from here. In 1981, Randall Lee Smith befriended two hikers, Robert Mountford and Laura Ramsay, on the trail. In the middle of the night, while the three slept at the shelter, Smith shot Robert in the head with a .22 bullet and, after a struggle, killed Laura in a gruesome stabbing. In a plea deal, he was convicted of two counts of second-degree murder for his crimes. After fifteen years behind bars, Smith was paroled in 1996. But in 2008, just miles from the site of the original attack, Smith attempted to kill two fishermen he met under similar circumstances. This time, however, the pair survived the attack, despite numerous gunshot wounds to the head, neck, and chest. Smith, however, did not. As he attempted to escape, he crashed his getaway truck. He survived long enough to be taken to prison before dying from the injuries he sustained.

I was a bit creeped out recalling this memory and, besides the fact that I had eaten pepperoni and cheese wrapped up in a tortilla for lunch numerous times on the hike, the food seemed tasteless, as if the spirits of those departed souls were affecting my appetite since they no longer had living desires for sustenance. We didn't linger, cutting our lunch break shorter than normal. I even left the last few bites of my lunch for the mice that inhabited the shelter and did not seem to be concerned with the incorporeal aura of the area.

As we continued to advance up the trail we came to the section known as the *Virginia Triple Crown*. The first of these was Dragon's Tooth. At the top of this climb was a rock formation that resembled a big dragon tooth. The formation itself was made of quartzite, and the tallest tooth rose about 35 feet above the mountain top. Some people climb it to the top, and yes, I am one of those people. I tied Sawyer off below and scaled it. Luckily for me, there was no one else around when this 50-something body attempted this. The climb required hand over hand maneuvering, and in several places I stopped to hold on for dear life. I'm sure the expression on my face might have been entertaining to some. When I got to the top, I was rewarded with an amazing view of the valley below, where you could see tiny houses nestled in along the mountainside. It was nice to get these views because when I was hiking on the trail, it was often in a green tunnel of trees with full leaf cover, and you can't see more than a few feet on either side.

The next in the triple crown was McAfee Knob. This was known as the most photographed spot on the entire Appalachian Trail. The green tunnel of trees fell back here and it opened up on a rocky plateau with fantastic views of the countryside below. There was one unique rock slab that jutted out over the 3000 foot drop to the valley floor. That was the feature that gave it the "knob" moniker. I'd been there before on a day hike but it was no less fantastic this time. Sawyer and I had our picture taken out on the knob by a day hiker who'd come up to enjoy the view. When we posed for the picture, I sat on the knob with my legs dangling over the edge, and Sawyer laid down right next to me with his nose inches (don't worry, I had him firmly under leash control) from the side. It remains one of my favorite pictures to this day.

Just down from McAfee Knob was Tinkers Cliff. An entire section of cliffs with each one providing more fabulous views of the tiny (from here) city of Daleville below. After more photos here, we hiked on until the trail deposited us in that town. I was excited, not only for the fantastic views we had just seen but because this was where we took our first zero day.

A zero day was a day you hike no trail miles. It's like a day off work. We rolled into town and got a room at the pet-friendly Super 8 motel. After showering and cleaning Sawyer properly this time, I walked 0.1 mile to a BBQ joint called Three Lil' Pigs. I smashed the hell out of some ribs, sausage, and chicken. I also knocked back several beers. It wasn't a fancy six course meal, but it tasted like a feast fit for a King, even if it only fed hiker trash. Pets weren't allowed inside, so I had to leave Sawyer at the motel. Don't worry, I didn't forget about him. There was no pet food in his future for dinner. I carried quite the literal doggy bag back for him, which he smashed himself in no time.

The next day I did a quick resupply from Krogers and did laundry at the motel. We spent the rest of the time relaxing. We watched TV, got caught up on social media, and the best part of all, is that I got to call my wife and have an extended conversation, instead of a quick *I only have one bar of service but we're still alive* call. I was able to catch up on what was going on at home and she was regaled with tales of our adventures so far. I was really thankful for having such a strong partner (and best friend, sorry Sawyer, she just edges you out) that could handle taking care of business at home while we walked in the woods all day. We didn't leave the motel for the rest of the day. Pizza was delivered for lunch and dinner. The next morning we got geared up, ate a free continental breakfast, then hit the trail.

Up and down mountains, we continued to hike. Camping at shelters or tent spots, ducking into towns to resupply, and having the time of our lives. Sometime later we crossed the James River on the longest footbridge on the AT. The bridge is foot traffic only and was built on the piers of a demolished train bridge that had been replaced. Just east of the footbridge was the new train bridge. While we were crossing and enjoying the view of the fast rushing river below, a train came across. When Sawyer saw the train he put his front paws up on the side of the footbridge rail and barked. The train engineer, visible from the open window in the locomotive, saw Sawyer's greeting and returned it with a blast from the train whistle.

Once across the river we got picked up by a driver from the Stanimal's Hostel in Glasgow. A former thru-hiker named Stan ran this hostel. His trail name was, naturally, Stanimal. I had never stayed in a hostel before, so I wanted to try it for the night. It was like a communal living experience. Your fee got you a bed in one room you shared with other hikers. I thought I might be a little uncomfortable in this environment but I found it pleasurable. You had full kitchen privileges and access to most of the areas in the house. There was a common room that all the hikers hung out in to watch TV, movies, and just shoot the shit. Sawyer was quite the hit there too, especially with the female hikers. I had only planned on staying for the night but I just couldn't get my rear in gear the next morning and ended up taking another zero there, lazing about, eating unhealthy food (but high in calories), and talking "hiker stuff" with my fellow hostel mates. One, who went by the trail name of Hippy Chick, told us of a bear encounter.

"I just came around a bend in the trail," she said. "And there he was. I was scarred but also excited. I got a few pictures with my phone, and then tried to scare him off by yelling and clacking my trekking poles. He didn't move. I yelled again and he started coming toward me. I turned to run."

"Oh no," several of us said in unison.

"I know, I know. Big no no. I remembered that a few seconds later and turned back around. The bear was coming. I screamed and waved my poles again. About ten feet away it stopped, looked at me for a second, snorted, and ran off the side of the trail into the trees."

"So he bluffed charged you?" I asked.

"Yup! Thank God that's all it was."

"I haven't seen a bear yet on this trip. Was kind of hoping I would."

"Well, when you get into the Shenandoah National Park, your chances will get better. There is a high concentration of bears there."

"Cool, although I can do without the bluff charges."

The following morning I pulled us from the suction of the vortex and we continued up the trail. Nothing of note happened in the next couple of weeks. We reached a point where it became a bit routine. There are sections of the trail that didn't have the great views, and it was more like a job to hike them. We got up, ate breakfast, struck camp, hiked, ate lunch at the best spot we could find, hiked some more, set up camp, ate dinner, and then went to bed by hiker's midnight. The next day we would repeat the process; *wash, rinse, repeat* for days at a time. We had to put our heads down and make it through these sections to get to the "good stuff". Don't get me wrong. While there was nothing special about hiking these sections, it certainly beat being in the city any day of the week, and twice on Sunday. Never fear, things got exciting again.

Sawyer

One day, after a tough climb, Dad tied me to a tree and climbed this big rock. It took him awhile to make it to the top, even with his fancy dancy opposable thumbs. He made it though. Later on we came to a place I remembered being before on a day hike. This time, however, we got another hiker to take our picture together out on the jutting rock. The cool breeze was blowing and ruffling my fur. It felt great and I was just glad to be there with Dad. I've heard Dad tell people that is one of his favorite pictures. It's my favorite too. He probably thinks I don't understand what it is when he shows other people on his phone, but I do.

A day later we went into town to have what Dad called a zero day. I wasn't sure what that meant, but I understood it when he said we wouldn't be hiking the next day. That was fine with me. My paws could use a break. I don't have hiking shoes, you know. What wasn't fine with me was when Dad told me I had to stay in the motel room while he went out.

What gives here Dad? I gave him my best hangdog face.

"Don't worry, buddy," he said to me. "I'll make it up to you."

I wondered what he meant by that? When he got back, I found out. A whole bag of meaty goodness! I devoured it with gusto.

On we hiked. We crossed this long bridge over a river. As we were crossing it, a big machine passed us on another bridge close by. I reared up on the railing to get a better look and gave it a good bark. Not sure why, just seemed like the appropriate thing to do. The machine barked back at me! Well, not exactly a bark, it was a whistle, but not the kind Dad occasionally blows to get my attention when I am straying too far on the long leash. This whistle was loud!

We took another ride in a van to a place with a bunch of people. All of them were cool and I hardly got to spend time with Dad because of all the attention showered on me by the other hikers. The women especially loved to give me ear scratches and belly rubs. It worked for me! We stayed there a day and a half. I could have stayed there even longer but Dad said we had to get back on the trail.

Dad

Sawyer and I were beat tired from crossing over a section of the trail called Three Ridges. It was tough ups and downs with a lot of rocks that were hard on the feet and nasty trip hazards. Up until this point I hadn't had a major fall, but coming down a steep rocky downgrade, my foot caught a rock and down I went. Like a pinball in a machine I used to play as a kid in the local arcade, I bounced and ricocheted off rocks and trees down the slope. As I zig zagged down, I wished someone would tilt this particular pinball machine so it would stop. My world had certainly been tilted off axis. Sawyer saw what was happening and pulled back hard on the leash, digging all four paws into the ground. If he hadn't done that I would have fallen much further and probably suffered a lot more damage. As it was, I had a good welt on the right side of my cheek where my head had bounced off a rock. I came to rest in a little thicket off a bend in the trail. I was lying on my backpack like an overturned turtle. I tried to right myself, but every time I grunted and heaved to the left or right, I would almost get there and then roll right back over! "This is regodamndiculous!" I shouted to no one in particular (maybe Mother Nature). However, Sawyer is the one that came to my rescue again. He encouraged me by licking my face and then pulled on the leash while I tried once again to turn my "shell" over. With the extra effort put in by Sawyer, I finally got myself back on the right side of the ground.

I got down on my banged up knees and draped my arms around Sawyer in a tight embrace. "Thanks boy! That could've been bad. Love you!" Sawyer normally doesn't go in for hugging, but this time he seemed to tolerate it.

As I was getting myself cleaned off, I noticed something was missing. Where was my walking stick? I looked all around and couldn't find it. Several feet off the trail from where I rested was a drop off. I carefully peeked over the side and ten feet down, on a ledge outcropping, was my stick. It was precariously balanced on the side of the ledge, half of it sticking out over the edge where it looked like about a 1000 feet drop to the valley below. Shit! A stiff breeze could upset that balance and my stick would be a goner.

I tied Sawyer off to a nearby tree and dropped my pack. I opened it up and withdrew my throwing rock bag. Inside was the para-cord. I tied a carabiner to the end of the cord and laid down on my belly, hanging slightly over the drop off. I wanted to lower the carabiner and get it latched on to the leather strap of my walking stick. On the first attempt, I let gravity take over and lowered the carabiner down to the ledge. That wasn't going to work. It came to rest near the ledge wall and too far away from the stick. I was going to have to throw it to get it next to the stick. It took me several tries but I finally got it close enough. As I pulled, the carabiner slid along and up against the strap. I gave a quick tug, hoping to snag the strap. The carabiner caught the strap but it didn't fully attach to it and popped loose, but not before upsetting the stick's position, causing it to swing out even further over the side of the ledge. I held my breath as I watched the stick move, thinking it was gone for sure. But the stick finally stopped moving and didn't go over.

I took in a big gulp of air. That was close! My heart was pumping fast and I felt my head swimming. When I steadied myself and got my courage back up, I retrieved the carabiner and tried another throw. That's when I really fucked up. The carabiner hit the part of the stick that was hanging over the edge. The stick upended and slid off the edge! I put both my hands over my head and buried it in the dirt, crying, "No!"

Off to the side of my head I could hear a weird noise, and I looked up. The excess para-cord was quickly unwinding as it ran over the drop off. Before I could react I saw a blur of gold as Sawyer pounced on the unspooling line with his front paws, then clamped down on it with his mouth.

"Good job!" I said to him. "At least you saved the cord and carabiner."

Then I saw that Sawyer struggled with the cord and it began to slip through his mouth, so I reached over and grabbed it. At seeing this, Sawyer let go and I noticed a much heavier weight than there should have been with just a carabiner tied to the end. I slowly wound the line back up and several seconds later I saw the top of my walking stick come up over the edge of the drop off. What the what? I grabbed the stick and hauled it all the way up. Firmly attached to the carabiner was the leather strap of my stick. When it went over the edge, the strap must have snagged the carabiner on the way down and caught. If it hadn't been for Sawyer's quick thinking, the stick, carabiner, and cord would all be a 1000 feet down right now.

I let out a loud *Woohoo* and tried to give Sawyer another hug, but he backed away. Guess his tolerance for hugging had been reached for the day. Instead, I broke out some doggy treats and let Sawyer have his fill (there is no tolerance level for this.) As an additional reward, I took his backpack and strapped it to mine. I'd take a little extra weight for a while in appreciation of having my walking stick back. I gripped the stick tightly and we set off up the trail again, satisfied that the situation hadn't been any worse than it could have been.

As we were coming down from Three Ridges, I was aching, but my spirits couldn't have been higher. Why is that you ask? At the bottom, the landscape opened up into a wide meadow that led to a road at Reeds Gap along the Blue Ridge Parkway. So what? Well, at the gap parking lot sat my Jeep, and in that Jeep sat my wife! We only lived about three hours from this spot and she had come to visit with us. We were going to spend three days in a cabin not too far from here that we often vacationed at.

It was the first time I had seen my wife since she dropped us off over a month ago in Damascus. You know the first thing she did? Bypassed my outstretched arms to cover Sawyer in kisses and hugs, which I guessed he'd raised his tolerance level for her. Instead of getting mad, I just laughed. It was typical of her. Besides, she made it up to me later that night, if you know what I mean.

We spent an awesome three zero days at the cabin on Love Mountain. That's a real place, I shit you not. The cabin was one of several at a resort called Royal Oaks just off the Blue Ridge Parkway that is a scenic drive along the ridgeline of the mountains. Ten years ago I found this place when I surprised my wife with a Valentine's Day weekend trip. When I was checking us in at the office the first time, I met the owner, Keith, who was giving me suggestions on things to do in the area.

"Do you like to hike?" he asked me.

I thought about it. I *did* like to hike, but I hadn't done any hiking for years at that time. I used to go on hikes when I lived out in California, but the daily grind of life had overtaken that activity. "I do like to hike," I told him, not getting into the details of the fact that I hadn't for quite a while.

Keith had pulled out a map and circled a local trail called Crabtree Falls that was a short few miles hike up to a spectacular water fall. I ended up taking that hike by myself. My wife was not up to it and Sawyer wasn't even a thought in his sire's mind yet. It was a nice hike and it got my juices for nature flowing again. Later on, I looked at the map that Keith had given me and noticed it was for a section of the Appalachian Trail with side trails in the area. I had once heard about the AT in passing but really knew nothing about it. This map got me interested and I started doing research online. That's where I discovered the culture of the trail and my obsession was born.

During our reunion zero days we grilled out, drank, played

board games, and even did a few small hikes as a family. One day we went back to Reeds Gap and did trail magic. Some hikers that stopped I had met before, and I enjoyed introducing them to my wife. I shuttled a few hikers down the mountain five miles to a microbrewery called Devil's Backbone. They made my favorite beer, Vienna Lager. I didn't waste a chance to load up on a big growler jug and bring it back to the cabin.

The break was great but seemed to fly by and Sawyer and I found ourselves at Oh-dark-thirty standing back in the parking lot at the trailhead waving goodbye to my wife again. I don't know why, but it seemed a lot harder to leave this time than it had back in Damascus. I guess the time apart had truly made the heart grow fonder. Nevertheless, our adventure was not over yet, so I tightened the waist strap on my pack and we hiked on north.

Sawyer

Weeks later we were hiking through some serious rocks when I saw Dad trip and fall! He bounced down the slope and I could see the leash running out of slack. The only thing I could think to do was dig in with all four paws and fight the forward tugging. It was quite the jerk on the leash, and the harness bit into my shoulders, but I slowed Dad down enough so he came to a stop.

Dad! Are you all right? I ran to where he was lying and licked his face. Once he got upright again (with more help from me) he thanked me, told me he loved me, and got down on his knees to give me a hug. I'm not a big hugger, but I allowed it this time. Besides, I have to confess that while I wanted to help him, my actions had been self-serving too. I didn't want to get dragged over the side of a mountain either.

I saw Dad frantically start searching around the area looking for something. What was he doing? He got some stuff out of his pack and then tied me off to a nearby tree. Then he laid down on his stomach and started fiddling with things over the edge. *Dad, what's going on here?* He didn't answer me, of course. I heard him shout, "No!" which startled me. Then I heard a whizzing noise and saw that the cord Dad used to do his inept bear bag hanging was slithering through the leaves on the ground. I still wasn't sure what was going on but my instinct took over and I leapt at the cord and got my front paws on it. Luckily, I was within leash range to accomplish this. I then clamped down on it with my teeth and stopped it from moving. I heard Dad say something to me but I didn't make it out because the cord in my mouth got heavy and started to slip out. Dad quickly grabbed the line and got it stopped again.

I let go of the cord and watched Dad wind it up until I saw something come up over the edge. Oh! It was his walking stick. It must have gone over the side when he fell. So I had saved his stick? It wasn't much use to me but I know Dad loved that thing. I was glad to help. In fact, unbeknown to me at the time, I had just saved my own life, but that's still up the trail a ways.

Dad gave me a bunch of treats as a reward and I enjoyed them, but the real treat was when he took off my backpack and carried it himself! Now that was some gratitude there! *Love you, Dad!*

A little while later we were following the trail through a meadow and it seemed familiar to me. Then I saw something I knew was familiar, our Jeep was parked there. Mom was running up the trail to embrace me! This must have been national hugging day, but I allowed this one too because I hadn't seen her in a long time. I looked over to where Dad was standing with his outstretched empty arms, and, if my anatomy had allowed it, I would have snickered. *Ha! She loves me more than you, pal!* I knew that wasn't true but I was going to play it up anyway.

We spent three glorious days at the cabin I had been to many times before. But all too soon it was over and Dad and I geared back up and prepared to say goodbye to Mom again. This time together had been really fun and I would miss Mom a lot, but I was also anxious to get back on the trail with Dad. He hooked up

LEE LOVELACE

my hiking leash and we set foot and paw on the path that led us to our further adventures.

CHAPTER THREE

Shenandoah National Park

Dad

That night we camped at the Paul Wolfe Shelter. This was actually the first shelter on the AT that Sawyer and I had seen several years ago on a day hike when we were staying at the cabin. It's a nicely built shelter, with two sleeping decks, and it had a fairly large stream running by. I pitched our tent next to the stream so we could listen to it babbling while we rested. There were three other hikers there, a father and son with trail names of Chief and Fire Bug, and a solo hiker, Stonewall. We had a good time sitting around a fire outside the shelter, cooking our meals and doing the hiker chat thing. Fire Bug, as you might imagine, built the fire for us.

"I'm taking a zero in Waynesboro tomorrow," Stonewall informed the group.

"Us too," replied Chief, as he indicated his son with a sweeping motion of his hand.

"Not us," I said. "We are heading into the SNP first thing in the morning." The SNP is the Shenandoah National Park.

"You're not even going into town to resupply and eat at the Chinese Buffet? I heard it's pretty sweet," Fire Bug said.

"Nope, we just spent three zero days in a row at a cabin just south of here with my wife. We went into town one day to resupply." The Chinese Buffet was a staple on the trail for many hikers. It was an all you can eat place that I heard had quality food. AYCE places were high on a hiker's list of preferred dining establishments. They did wonders to assuage hiker hunger. "I wish we could try the buffet out, but the logistics didn't work out this time. I'll eat there one day."

The next day Sawyer and I stood in front of a little kiosk at the entrance to SNP. Thru and section hikers didn't have to pay an entrance fee to enter the park but you had to fill out a permit form and drop it into a collection box. They also require you to tie a carbon copy of the form on your backpack so any ranger that stopped you could easily inspect it. That was cool with me, but I wondered what would happen to the paper copy when it rained? Well, it wasn't raining now, so I didn't worry about it. Sawyer wasn't required to carry one on his pack, that slacker.

With the form in the box and the copy affixed to my pack, we hiked into the park. One advantage of the park was that it crossed the Skyline Drive many times. The Skyline Drive was a scenic road that ran the 105 mile length of the park. What's so great about a road when you're hiking? Well, there are waysides along this road where you can get some food that hadn't been freeze-dried and sitting beside my dirty socks. We wouldn't be required to carry as much food, and any reduction in weight was a welcome thing for me, and I'm betting Sawyer too, although he only carried his snacks and water in his Outward Hound pack.

"Hey, in a few days we're going to be close to where you were born," I informed Sawyer. He looked at me with a puzzled expression on his face. Sawyer had been born at the Colebrook Golden Retriever breeding farm in Harrisonburg, just to the west of the park and a little more north of our current position. "Should we stop by and pay a visit to your Mom and Dad?" He looked even more confused so I let it drop.

We hiked into the park. The grades seemed easier here and we enjoyed the smooth sailing. After a while we arrived at a clearing where there were communications antennas and a small building below that I assumed was a control station. Next to the building sitting in a field were, honest to God, tractor seats planted in the ground. Now that's not something you see every day. I had to get a selfie sitting in one of those. I tried to get Sawyer to sit in one, but he wasn't interested. I did get him to sit by my side as I snapped a picture.

That night we camped at the Calf Mountain Shelter and we were the only ones there. I think the main bubble of hikers I had been around were all in Waynesboro right now. The cool thing was, there was a bear pole at this site. Instead of doing a bear bag hang in a tree, you could lift your bag up to the top of the pole with a long stick and place it on one of the several hooks that were out of critters' reach.

Since we were alone and it was supposed to rain that night, I decided we would stay in the shelter. Staying at a shelter can be tricky with Sawyer, even when no one else is there, because I can't leave him off leash like I can in the tent. I'm sure he doesn't mean to run away, but sometimes his curiosity gets the best of him and he goes off wandering. Luckily, the picnic table at the shelter was right up near the entrance and I tied the long leash off to it and still had enough slack so he could sleep next to me. Except for him deciding to get all tangled up once during the night, we made out all right.

The rain started coming down hard around 4 AM, but we stayed nice and dry in the shelter. It was still raining when we woke in the morning and I was thankful I didn't have to pack up a wet tent. We had a quick cold breakfast of Pop Tarts and then I put on my rain suit and off we went. The rain suit did a good job of keeping the rain off me but it caused me to sweat something awful and in no time I was just as soaked as if I hadn't worn it at all.

The rain came down steadily and made for a miserable day hiking. I wondered why I enjoyed hiking on days like that. But then I thought days like that were what made the other days so enjoyable. It was just something we had to push through to get to the good days. We ate a somewhat dry lunch sitting in the Blackrock Hut shelter. I briefly considered just calling it a day but we had only gone thirteen miles and I felt we had a lot more left in the tank, even with the rain. So we pushed on.

The rain finally let up around 4:00 o'clock and at 5:00 we came upon the Loft Mountain Campground. This was a campground accessible to cars from Skyline Drive. Looking at my guide, I learned it was mostly set up for car campers but there were several sites close to the trail more suited for hikers. I hadn't planned on stopping here, other than checking out their camp store, but we had hiked 20 miles today, which was our longest yet. The next shelter was still six miles away and we were beat.

"What do you say Sawyer? Want to call it a day and stay here?" Sawyer gave me a solitary, sharp bark. "I'll take that as a yes."

With the backing of Sawyer, I didn't think twice about shelling out $15 for one spot near the trail.

Sawyer

Dad said something about the place I was born. I could vaguely recall being in a pen with my brothers and sisters, but that comment about seeing my Mom and Dad I didn't get either. The only Dad I knew was standing right here, and Mom had dropped us off at the trail the other day. I looked at him and after a second he hiked on and I followed.

We eventually came to a clearing and there were these seat thingies sticking in the ground. Dad got all excited about it. He sat down and started taking pictures of himself, and then he tried to get me to get up in one. *Not happening, bud!* I eventually agreed to sit by him as he took a picture just so we could get moving. We were in an open field with the sun shining down and I was getting hot. I wanted to get back into the cover of the trees and the shade they provided.

That night we stayed in a shelter instead of the tent. Shelters weren't my favorite because I didn't feel all that secure with the open side like I did in the tent. Plus, there were overwhelming scents of mice in here. One of those beady-eyed pests better not show his face while I was around. When it was time to go to sleep, I curled up next to Dad and drifted off quick. However, in the night I woke to the sound of something scrounging around outside the shelter. I also detected a scent that I had smelled before but never attached to anything. I looked over to Dad, and heard him snoring away.

Guess it was up to me to investigate this situation. I got up and went to the edge of the shelter. I saw nothing but I could still smell it. I hopped down from the shelter and started roving around the site to check things out. I could only get so far from the shelter because Dad tied the long leash to the table in front. That's when I saw what was making the noise. It was big and black and furry. It had huge paws and a mouth full of teeth. I'd seen one before, but not this close up. Yup, it was a bear and it was trying to climb up the pole to get to our food bag. I'm not going to lie, yes dogs can lie, especially to themselves, but I was scared shitless. I had never been close enough to associate them with their scent. This one was plenty close to attach a scent to it. Too close! But I was supposed to protect Dad, so I started barking, and baring my teeth at the bear.

The bear looked startled and took off running around the other side of the shelter. I tried to follow it just to make sure it was gone but in all my roving around I had tangled the leash up in the legs of the table and I couldn't get loose. I just continued to bark to make sure the bear knew to keep on running. That's when Dad woke up.

"Sawyer! What the hell?" He came out and got me untangled, all the while muttering curses under his breath. He had no clue a bear had just been visiting and trying to help himself to our food.

"Now get in the shelter and lie down," he told me. *Thanks for the gratitude, Dad. Sheesh.*

The next day we hiked in the rain. It wasn't my favorite thing in the world to do. I had to shake my head to clear the rain from my eyes. It kept me cool though, and that was alright with me.

Later on, the rain stopped and we came to a place with a bunch of people camped.

"What do you say Sawyer? Want to call it a day and stay here?" Dad asked me. I was beat and would love to do just that. *Yes!* I said, and since I knew he couldn't hear that, I added one bark that I hoped he would understand as my affirmative vote. Guess I got my point across because that's where we stayed the night. If we had just kept going for a bit we might not even have had a reason to tell this story.

CHAPTER FOUR

Ranger Dick

Dad

I picked out a site that was fifty yards from the trail. It was a nice set-up with a tent pad, table, and a fire pit. The best thing of all was that there was a bear box. It was a hefty metal box that you could lock up all your stuff in to keep them out of the reach of the critters. No bear bag hang for me tonight! I set the tent up on the pad, which looked ridiculously small since they constructed it for much bigger tents. After getting out the water bottles, I tossed my whole backpack in the bear box, then Sawyer and I walked to find the rangers' station to pay for the site.

Along the way we passed a bathroom. A bathroom with running water and flushing toilets even! I took advantage of these hiker amenities, filling up our water bottles and doing my business in something other than a privy or a hole dug in the woods. After that stop, we continued on to the rangers' station. The young ranger there was a pleasant fellow and gave us a sheet of the rules for the campground. One of those was quiet hours began at 10 PM. I laughed at this thinking we'd be long asleep by then. We headed back to our site and I set about getting organized and ready to cook dinner.

On the sheet of rules, it stated dogs had to be on a leash no longer than six feet. This was a bit of a problem since Sawyer's camp leash was much longer than six feet. I didn't want to leave

43

him on his hiking leash because at its furthest expansion it was only four feet. So as a compromise, I tied a knot around the leg of the bear box so that only six feet of the long leash was free, and hooked Sawyer to it. He tested the new length of his leash and he did not at all look happy about it.

"Sorry bud," I said to him. "Rules are rules."

I made a Mountain House meal to celebrate our twenty mile day. While I was preparing things, Sawyer finally accepted his situation and plopped down to chill out. I had just poured the water into the stove pot and was about to hit the striker button when I heard a noise from up the trail that led down from the parking lot to our site. A green-clad ranger was approaching. This was an older guy, not the one I had seen up at the rangers' station. Sawyer heard him coming too and stood up. As Ranger Rick (my wife and I always called them this due to the Ranger Rick magazines we read as kids) strolled into our camp, Sawyer eyed him closely and uttered a single "Woof." Not even a full on bark. Just a very low non-threatening "Woof."

Ranger Rick lost his shit. He pulled out a can of mace from a holster on his utility belt and aimed it at Sawyer. Then he yelled, "Restrain your animal! Restrain your animal!"

I was shocked. Sawyer was just standing there staring at him. Ranger Rick moved closer to Sawyer so I jumped up and ran over and grabbed the leash. "He's leashed," I told Ranger Rick and showed him.

He re-holstered his mace, then said sternly, "Dogs must be on no longer than a 6 foot leash!"

OK, now I might see his concern if he saw the excess portion of the long leash lying on the ground. "I understand. I tied his long leash off to the bear box so he wouldn't have more than six feet to roam." I showed this by pulling on the leash connected to Sawyer and showing him it came up no longer than six feet from the knot I had tied to the leg of the box.

Ranger Rick looked at it for a second and then, as if deciding he didn't want his authority challenged, said, "Doesn't matter. He can't be on a leash longer than six feet, no matter what. Do you have a shorter leash? If not, I have the authority to eject you from this campground."

Eject us? Really? "I have his hiking leash which is only four feet, but..."

"You'll have to use that then."

I could see there would be no negotiating with this guy, so I dragged Sawyer's hiking leash off the table and switched it out with the long one. Now he was glued to the side of the bear box.

"You can't hook him to the bear box either," he said to me after I had hooked him to the bear box.

For Christ's sake! I half wished Sawyer *had* bitten him! I unhooked Sawyer from the bear box and re-hooked him to one of the table legs. The poor guy could only just go under the table and lay down.

Ranger Rick spoke up again, "I was coming down to tell you that we had a lot of bear activity near the campground lately so, keep your food and scented items locked in the bear box."

"OK," I told him, not wanting to prolong the conversation. Most rangers I had met in my previous hiking trips were pleasant and I liked talking to them. Not this guy.

He looked at me again like I wasn't taking him seriously. I felt like telling him I had been out on the trail for almost two months and knew how to keep my stuff bear free. I didn't though, because I had a feeling he wouldn't take that kindly and I just wanted this encounter over with.

"Just so you know," he said. "I have the authority to eject you from this campground if you don't follow the bear safety rules."

Again with this authority to eject us shit? "No problem," I said.

"Are you backcountry camping?"

"Sure am. We're on a section hike along the AT."

"Where's your permit?"

OK, he couldn't bitch about this one. My pack was leaning against the table and I fished inside one of my hip belt pockets and produced the permit. He looked at it for a second and then handed it back to me.

45

"You know you're supposed to carry that attached to the outside of your pack."

"I know, but it was raining today and I didn't want it to get destroyed. Then I wouldn't have a permit to show you."

He looked at me like my father used to look when I back talked him. "Attach it to the outside of your pack." Man this guy was a dick! He moved to another campsite, but before he was gone he looked back over his shoulder and said, "Keep that animal under control or I'll…" *Eject us from the park,* I thought in my head as he said the same thing out loud.

That's when I pegged this asshole. He was the kid in school that got picked on a lot. He grew up and got a little bit of positional authority and let it go to his head. He was going to get back at the world for treating him like shit when he was a kid by showing us he was the big man on campus now.

I looked at Sawyer huddled miserably under the table. "Don't worry buddy, we'll eat a quick dinner and then get in the tent so you don't have to hang out under there." He showed me the enthusiasm for that plan by uttering one sharp bark! "Shhh!" I told him. "You don't want Ranger *Dick* coming back over here to eject us from this campground!" At that, I started laughing and Sawyer held his mouth open in a toothy grin. If he could, I am sure he would've been laughing along with me. We ate dinner, stuffed the bear box, and got in the tent to call it a night.

Sawyer

What's the deal with this short ass leash dad? He had just put my long leash on, but I couldn't go very far, certainly not as far as I could usually wander out.

"Rules are rules," he said to me.

Well, these rules suck! I stomped around to show my dissatisfaction, then I slumped down to the ground to sulk. I was not a happy camper. Dad set about to make dinner, but even the thought of some chow did little to improve my mood.

A few minutes later, I heard some noise from up the trail that led to our campsite and saw a guy approaching. I stood up to get a better look at this guy. I got a tingle and my hackles stood up. This is the sixth sense I was talking about when I met someone and knew they weren't a good person. I was already in a bad mood and now seeing this guy made me even more irritable. I wanted to let Dad know that this was a suspicious character, so I gave just the softest "woof" of a bark.

This guy went crazy. He started yelling and pointing something at me. Really dude? You're losing it because I gave you a single solitary "woof"? After he had Dad leash me to the table, I gave the dude a look of utter disgust and plopped down. I stared him down, not taking my eyes off this unpleasant individual.

Dad continued to talk to this guy and I could tell it was not a pleasant conversation. When the dude finally went away, Dad told me we would eat a quick dinner and get in the tent so I could get off the short leash. This sounded just find to me and I let him know my concurrence with that plan with one bark. Dad shushed me and told me not to make the dude come back, but he called him Ranger Dick. I thought that was hilarious. So did Dad because he started laughing and if I was built to laugh I would have done it too. I can grin though, and I gave him one of my best.

CHAPTER FIVE

Ancestral Instinct

Dad

The next morning we got up earlier than usual because we were anxious to put some distance between us and Ranger Dick. We were all packed up and just about to hit the trail when I heard footsteps. I turned around expecting to see Ranger Dick here to give us one last lecture, but it wasn't him. It was another guy I recognized from the campsite next to ours. Sawyer walked up to him (so I knew he was a good guy) but couldn't get there because he was attached to the four foot hiking leash.

"Hey," the guy said. "My name's Matt. Are you a thru-hiker?"

"No," I replied. "We are section hiking the AT through Virginia to Harper's Ferry."

"Ah, LASHers then."

This guy knew his terms so I assumed he had some backpacking experience. I walked closer so Sawyer could say hi. Matt bent down and petted him for a bit. "Yup, LASHers indeed," I told him. "This is the longest hike we've ever attempted."

"Well, my boyfriend, Chuck, and I would like to invite you over for some breakfast before you take off this morning."

Wow, some unexpected trail magic after the unpleasantness of Ranger Dick the day before? The trail runs close to the camp store on the other side of the campground and I had planned on stopping in there to get us a breakfast treat, but this sounded

48

much better. Sign me up! "That would be awesome. Thank you!"

We joined Matt and Chuck at the table at their site. Matt looked to be in his late 30's or early 40's, with close cropped black hair and a stocky frame. Chuck was taller and probably a little older, with almost the same hairstyle, though there were some streaks of gray in it. They were avid backpackers also, but had never thru-hiked either. They were car camping at Loft Mountain for a week so they could go on day hikes along the AT and the side trails in the area. They had a Coleman stove and cooked up a mess of scrambled eggs and sausages for our feast. Sawyer looked especially happy not to be eating dry food for breakfast. During our conversation, I related our encounter with Ranger Dick the day before.

"Yeah, that guy!" Chuck said. "He berated us because we accidentally left a bottle of Vitamin I on the table when we went out on a hike yesterday." Vitamin I was what hikers call Ibuprofen. It was commonly used to assuage the aches and pains of hiking, so it's more like a daily vitamin. "Guess he was worried that all the bears that stole beer would need it for their hangovers."

We all busted up laughing at that one. "Yeah that guy's a dick," I said. "That's why Sawyer and I call him Ranger Dick!" That elicited another round of laughter. We chatted for a bit, but I felt the vortex pulling us in, so I thanked them for the trail magic and we set off up the trail.

We stopped in at the camp store and did a resupply. The prices here were outrageous, but I didn't have a choice as we were running low on food. However, I did splurge and got Sawyer a beef jerky treat, and for me? I got a tall boy Bud Lite beer. I stuffed the can in my pack to drink it later when we camped for the night. Sure, it was going to be warm by then but, you know, beer.

After that stop, we finally got back on the trail and started doing some miles. About two miles up the trail, we came to a creek crossing the path. It was flowing well and I would have to rock hop it across. Sawyer never rock hopped. He just went full bore through creeks in his way. He stayed with me though and knew not to pull me off the rocks. As we crossed, I put my walking stick down on what I thought was a firm footing, but when I shifted my weight to the stick to prepare for a hop, it slipped out from under me and down I went, right into the creek. It didn't really hurt but I was on my hands and knees right in the middle of it soaked up to my thighs.

I stood up and noticed my stick was gone. I looked around for a few seconds before spotting it floating away downstream! I tried to go after it, but Sawyer's leash had gotten all tangled up in the rocks and was preventing me from moving. I quickly unbuckled my pack straps and threw it up on the bank, then I got Sawyer untangled and clicked his leash around a small limb on a little tree growing by the creek. Free of that and the weight of my pack I stumbled through the water after my stick. Luckily, I only had to go about fifty yards downstream before I discovered that it had gotten caught up in some roots from an overhanging tree. I untangled and retrieved it, hugging it to my chest. That was the second time I almost lost my stick.

I was halfway back up the creek when I saw Sawyer standing up and staring intently at something upstream. From where I was I couldn't make out what he was looking at. With lighting speed, he took off after something. When he reached the four foot length of the leash, it didn't slow him down. The paltry limb I had hurriedly attached him to broke off like a twig in a hurricane. Oh shit! He was unrestrained and running off into the woods! I ran as fast as I could through the creek and finally up on to the bank to follow his path. Bushwhacking through the undergrowth slowed me down but after coming around a bend in the creek I got in view of Sawyer in just enough time to see him launch and tackle a small deer that had stopped to get a drink from the creek!

Sawyer got the deer around the throat and shook it violently. "Sawyer! Stop!" I yelled. But it was no use; he was in full predator instinct mode now. I had seen him take down birds, squirrels, rabbits, and opossums, but I had never seen him get something this large compared to his size. He continued to violently thrash the deer as I made my way over to him. The poor deer never stood a chance. By the time I got there, Sawyer had ripped its throat out and the deer (a doe from what I could make out) had the glazed over eyes of death. I grabbed the leash and pulled Sawyer back. At first he resisted hard, but then he finally calmed down, looked at me, and gave me a bloody grin as if to say *Look what I got, Dad!*

Sawyer

Dad and I were hiking along and I was still licking my lips, thinking about that trail magic breakfast that those two guys gave us. I could have gone for a couple more helpings of that! But even what I got was better than the dry food I usually ate for breakfast. We came up to a creek and I started across. Dad was hopping on the rocks, trying not to get his feet wet. I don't know why he doesn't just walk through it like me. It was much easier than all that hopping. I was leading the way and I heard a commotion and felt a sharp tug on my leash. Looking back, I saw Dad on his hands and knees right in the middle of the creek. It was a hilarious sight! However, Dad didn't look like he felt the same. Once he got up he started looking around frantically and I couldn't figure out what the problem was. He unbuckled his pack and threw it up on the bank, then took me and tied me off to a small tree. What was he doing?

I saw him scramble off down the creek and he disappeared around a bend. *Uhm, OK, I'll just wait here, I guess.* A scent caught my nose. What was that? I've smelled it before. It belonged to one of those spindly legged creatures with spots on their hide. I looked around and spotted one upstream getting a drink. Then a red lust overtook me. I could no more deny it than I could deny breathing. I had to have this creature.

Not even thinking about the leash, I shot off along the side of the creek. I barely felt a tug when the leash became taught for just a second before snapping loose and coming with me. As fast as I could, I made a beeline for the creature. I'd chased all kinds of creatures before, and while I had caught some, most of them, especially ones this far from me, usually took off before I could get them. Not this creature, though. It looked up at the noise of my galloping approach and just stared inquisitively for a few seconds. This was all the time I needed. The creature sensed danger and turned to flee, but I was on it! I wasn't even thinking now, just following my instinct. I bit down on the creature's neck and thrashed it violently! It squealed a few times, but then went silent and still. I tasted its hot blood in my mouth, which just flamed the desire more. I clamped down harder and pulled back, ripping a chunk from the creature's neck.

I felt a hard tug from behind and realized that Dad was yelling and pulling on my leash. My instinct was to pull away and get back to my kill, but Dad kept pulling and calling my name. I finally acquiesced and stopped pulling. I looked at the creature and got a swell of pride. I'd never brought down anything so big. Grinning, I faced Dad. *Look what I got!*

CHAPTER SIX

No Good Deed Goes Unpunished

Dad

I looked at the scene for a few minutes. Dead deer lying on the ground with its throat ripped out. My hundred pound dog standing there with the deer's blood all over his face. Oh dear, what am I going to do? I got some water from the creek and wiped off Sawyer's maw. He wasn't too fond of that and kept squirming to get loose and get back to the deer. It was frustrating, but I couldn't be fully mad at him. His predator instincts had taken over. He couldn't help himself. However, I'd have to do something. Deer were a protected species in the national park. That's what made them so docile around men. On past hikes in the SNP, I had walked within five feet of these deer without them giving me so much as a glance. They didn't feel threatened. That cost this deer its life. I needed to at least report what had happened to the park rangers. I'm sure they'd understand.

I tied Sawyer off to a much sturdier tree this time and then moved the deer a little way from the creek. Sawyer tried his hardest to break the leash but it wasn't happening this time. I needed to get him away from here so he could calm down. I reattached his leash to my belt and played tug of war with him while leading him back to the trail. It took a few minutes with

53

him resisting all the way, but I finally got him there. I got the number for the local ranger station from my trail guide and pulled out my phone. But when I took it off airplane mode, I couldn't get a signal. This didn't surprise me as the creek we were standing by was in a valley. We were getting ready to head up a 400 foot climb. I would try again at the top.

I donned my pack, and we started up. The further away we got, the more Sawyer calmed down and got back into the rhythm of hiking. When we reached the summit, I checked my phone again. I had two bars so I dialed the number. The call went through and someone answered.

"Simmons Gap Ranger Station," the voice said.

"Hi. I'm out hiking the Appalachian Trail with my dog," I started off. "There was an incident." I didn't know quite how to explain it.

"What kind of incident?"

I figured there was only one way to say it. "My dog got loose and killed a deer. I just wanted to let someone know."

"I see. Where did this happen?"

I consulted my Guthook app and then said, "At Ivy Creek."

"Is the deer on the trail?"

"No, it's upstream a bit."

"Well, we are going to need to locate it and the best way would be for you to show us." I heard some papers shuffling and then the voice came back on the line. "Can you meet a ranger at the Ivy Creek Overlook where the trail comes out at the parking lot?"

I consulted the app again and saw that was less than a mile ahead. I really didn't want to hike there and then have to backtrack to the creek, but to keep in the good graces of the park, I would. "Sure, that's only a little under a mile from here."

"OK, a ranger will meet you there. Thanks for calling it in."

"No problem."

I disconnected the call, and we hiked. In no time we came out at the overlook right off Skyline Drive. There was parking space for five vehicles and a waist high rock wall separating the lot from the edge of the mountain. Motorist on Skyline Drive could pull over to take a gander at the scenery below. At that moment, there were no vehicles of any type there, so I sat down on the wall and waited. Sawyer sat at the base of the wall beside me and we had a snack.

Five minutes later I saw a green and white park truck pull off the Skyline Drive and into the overlook parking lot. When the truck had been parked the man inside got out and much to my dismay, it was Ranger Dick. Why? Why did it have to be that jackhole?

Ranger Dick came over and I could see the recognition in his eyes. He didn't acknowledge it though, he just said, "Heard you had a little trouble on the trail."

"Yes," I replied and related the same information that I had given the person at the ranger station.

"OK, let me get some stuff and then you can take me there." He was already equipped with everything he had when I had encountered him before, so I wondered what else he needed. He went back to the truck and pulled out a small day pack, in which he put some bottled water, and what seemed to be a strange looking small gun. He already had a service pistol on his belt, so I was wondering what this was.

"What's that?" I asked.

He looked at me like he didn't owe me any explanation but then sighed and said, "It's a tranquilizer gun. There already may be predators getting the scent of the dead dear. We don't want to kill any more animals if we can help it." With that statement he gave a sideways glance at Sawyer. This annoyed the hell out of me, but I said nothing. I wanted to get this unpleasant business over with as quickly as possible so we could get back to hiking.

We all headed back south on the trail and I couldn't help but notice that Ranger Dick was doing a lot of huffing and puffing like I had done at the beginning of the hike way back in Damascus. Guess he didn't go too many places that truck of his couldn't carry him. Sawyer and I both slowed our pace, and we hiked the rest of the way in silence.

When we got back to Ivy Creek, I tied Sawyer to another

sturdy tree so he wouldn't get all agitated at the sight of the deer. Then I led Ranger Dick up to where the dead deer lay. No predators had as of yet discovered it. Ranger Dick bent down and studied the deer and its fatal wound. He then stood up and made some notes on a map he had brought. He walked back down to the creek and I followed.

"We'll have some trail runners come down and get the carcass," he said.

"OK," I replied. "We are going to get back to hiking then." My plans were to pick up the pace and separate ourselves from Ranger Dick so we could leave all this nastiness in our rear-view mirror. I went over to the tree and unhooked Sawyer, intending to attach him back to my belt.

"We have one more bit of business to attend to first," I heard Ranger Dick say.

I was looking down, trying to find the loop on my belt for Sawyer's leash. When I looked up, I saw Ranger Dick standing with the tranquilizer gun drawn from his pack. I got a sense of dread and asked, "What business?"

"I have to take custody of your dog."

"What?"

"He killed a protected animal in the park. He's a dangerous animal and we can't have him in the park."

"He was just acting on instinct to hunt prey. He's not dangerous to other people."

"Nevertheless, I have to take him in."

"That's not necessary. We can leave the park." I didn't want to skip any part of the trail but I would do it for Sawyer's sake.

"I don't think you understand. He has to be taken in and put down."

"WHAT?" I yelled. This could not be happening. Surely this dick was just flexing his muscles to fuck with me but I couldn't take the chance. What was I going to do?

"Enough talk!" Ranger Dick screamed. "Give me the leash or I'll have to sedate him."

He raised the pistol, and that's when *my* instinct took over.

The instinct of a father protecting his offspring. I dropped Sawyer's leash and yelled, "Run, Sawyer!"

Sawyer didn't hesitate. He heard the seriousness in my voice and took off up the trail. Ranger Dick brought the tranquilizer gun up to get a bead on Sawyer as he was scrambling up the trail. It only took me a second to realize what I had to do. I quickly snatched up my walking stick that was leaning against my pack on the ground. That stick that had almost been lost twice on this trip. I took one step and brought the stick down hard on the arm of Ranger Dick that was holding the gun. I heard a satisfying crack and Ranger Dick dropped the gun.

I looked back to see Sawyer had disappeared around a bend in the trail, getting away clean. I turned back to see Ranger Dick fumbling with his injured arm, trying to get his service pistol out of its holster. He cleared the gun and got it halfway up. I had no choice. I swung the stick again and connected it with the side of his head. Another loud crack and he went down to the ground on his hands and knees, the pistol flying from his hand. He was obviously dazed but he was not out. He tried to unsnap a radio on his belt. If he got that out and made a distress call it would all be over. Well, in for a penny, in for a pound. I raised the stick and brought it down on the top of his head. This time he fell flat and did not move.

Sawyer

"Run, Sawyer!"

Dad dropped my leash and I could tell bad things were happening. Ranger Dick was pointing something at me that did not look good. I was getting the hell out of there! I took off running up the trail with my hiking leash dragging behind me. I hoped it didn't snag on anything. I risked one quick glance back and saw Dad fighting with Ranger Dick. Should I go back and help him? I was conflicted but Dad *had* told me to run and I could sense that my presence caused the trouble. I decided I would keep going and sort this all out later.

Soon I was around a bend and out of sight. I kept running up the trail, which was increasing in elevation. It was tiring me out but I wouldn't stop until I felt I was out of danger. I got to the top of the mountain, and stopped for a few minutes to catch my breath. I could have really used some water, but it was in my hated backpack and I couldn't get to it. Damn these stupid paws! I still didn't feel like I was out of trouble yet, so I kept going.

I came back out at the parking lot where we had met Ranger Dick before. Nobody was there at the moment and I just wandered around wondering what to do. As I did, I saw a car pull into the parking lot. I didn't know if these were good or bad people but I wouldn't hang around to find out. Not wanting to head back the way I had come, I took off up the trail again. I continued to follow the trail as it gained some more elevation and then did a steep drop. By the time I was at the bottom, I was parched.

Here, there was another trail that led away from the main one. When I sniffed that way I could barely detect the smell of water. I didn't hesitate. That's the way I would go. I hiked just a few minutes before I saw a shelter like we had stayed at many times before. I was experienced enough to know that where there was a shelter there was usually water, and this was no exception. A stream flowed right before you got to the shelter. I ran to the stream and drank to my heart's content. That's when I felt a tug on my leash and heard, "What do we have here?"

CHAPTER SEVEN

On The Run

Dad

What had I done? I had attacked a National Park Ranger! He had left me no choice. No way was I going to let him touch Sawyer. I bent down to examine Ranger Dick where he lay on the trail. I had a momentary twinge of guilt for still thinking of him as Dick when I had just brained him, but only momentarily, he *had* just tried to take my dog to kill him. I could see he was still breathing by the steady rise and fall of his chest. I put two fingers on his carotid artery to check his pulse just in case. It seemed to beat fine. At this point he groaned and it startled me. I quickly scanned the area and saw his service pistol lying under a Rhododendron bush on the side of the trail.

I quickly snatched up the gun and examined it. I'm no stranger to guns. I served 10 years in the military and have been around guns my whole life. I recognized this gun as a Sig Sauer P229. I half racked back the slide to make sure there was a round already chambered and then let it spring forward again. I then cocked the hammer all the way and turned back to Ranger Dick. He was still on the ground, unmoving. I pointed the gun at him anyway and after a few seconds when I was sure he wasn't coming to, I de-cocked the hammer and stuck the gun in the waistband of my hiking pants.

I could hear soft moans coming from Ranger Dick but he

didn't look like he would awaken soon. I had to get out of there and go find Sawyer. Before I did, however, I was going to help myself to a few of Dick's belongings. I already had his gun. To my collection I added the tranquilizer gun and the radio. I put these items in my pack and hoisted it on my back. I left the gun in my waistband, just in case. As I was getting ready to go I thought of something else. I bent back down to Ranger Dick and rummaged in his pockets. He moaned a little more at this but I found what I was searching for. I pulled his keys out and put them in my pocket. Hopefully, without a radio and keys to his truck, that would give me a little more time to figure out what I was going to do.

Right now, what I was going to do was get the fuck out of there and go find Sawyer. I left Ranger Dick where he was, grabbed my trusty walking stick, and headed north again at the fastest pace I could go with the added weight I was now carrying. Through the whole climb back up the mountain, all kinds of scenarios were playing out in my head and none of them ended well. By the time I reached the summit, I had one prevalent thought. No matter what ended up happening, it would probably be worse if I had this gun in my possession when it did.

I bushwhacked my way off the trail about a hundred yards and came to a cliff. Looking over the side, I could see it was a long way down. I pulled the gun out of my waistband and prepared to throw it over the side. But I didn't. It looked remote at the bottom of the cliff, but what if there was a way to reach that spot I didn't see? What if there was some other side trail that led to that spot? I couldn't help but feel responsible for leaving a loaded gun for anyone to pick up. What if a kid got hurt, or hurt someone else? No, I couldn't do that.

I pressed the magazine release on the gun and caught it as it slid out. I ejected all the bullets from the magazine, and then racked the slide on the gun to eject the bullet that had been in the chamber. I put all the bullets back in my pocket. I could have just chunked the gun now, but I didn't even want to take the chance of someone finding the gun and loading it with their own bullets. So I decided to field strip it and throw away the individual pieces. I had never field stripped a P229 before, but I had done it for several other guns. The idea behind it was basically the same with a few different actions for each model. After studying the gun for several seconds and a few trial and error moves, I figured out the process. I cocked the slide back and locked it in place. Then I pulled down on a takedown lever. After this, I released the slide and walked it all the way off the frame of the gun. I removed the recoil spring and the barrel of the gun. I now had five different parts of the gun in pieces.

I threw each part over the side in a different trajectory to land them as far apart from each other as possible. I figured this would drastically decrease the odds of anyone finding all the parts and putting them together. I also thought about throwing the tranquilizer gun over the side but held on to that one. Ranger Dick's keys took a trip over the side too, and then I headed back on the trail. As I was going down the mountain, I would periodically toss a bullet from my pocket into the woods on either side of the trail. By the time I was down, the bullets were gone.

I came up on the Ivy Creek Overlook again, hoping to see Sawyer hanging out here. But a quick scan showed nothing but Ranger Dick's truck parked where we had left it. There were no other vehicles, no other people, and no dogs. The only thing I could think to do was continue up the trail. I ascended again for a couple hundred feet, then started on a steep downhill section. In all this time I had not encountered one other person, which was a blessing. I barreled my way down the hill, barely taking the time to check my downward motion. I was anxious to find Sawyer and going way too fast. I almost ended up on my ass at least a half dozen times, but with the help of my walking stick, I managed to keep upright. This action was torture on my knees, even with the braces, and by the time I reached the bottom they were screaming in agony. This forced me to slow my pace down a bit and I continued on.

LEE LOVELACE

In a short time, I came upon an intersection. It was the turnoff to the Pinefield Hut. Now I had a decision to make. My decision was to figure out what choice Sawyer had made. Did he continue on the AT north, or turn down toward the shelter? My instinct told me he would stick to the main trail like he normally did. I usually had to course correct him when we left the main trail. OK, that seemed like the best option. I headed north and reached to pull out my water bottle for a drink. That's when I realized I only had a few sips left. Damn! I forgot! This is where I had planned to refill on water for the next leg of the hike. I couldn't go off looking for Sawyer with nothing to drink.

This delay frustrated me, but I had no choice. I backtracked and turned down the side trail to hike the 0.1 mile to the hut. I picked up my pace and I could hear the babbling of the stream near the shelter where I would refill. As I came around the bend, I saw a most curious sight. Not the stream. It was what was on the other side. There stood Matt and Chuck, the guys we had breakfast with that morning. It was also a glorious sight, because Matt was holding on to Sawyer's harness as he sat next to the couple! When Sawyer saw me he broke out of Matt's grasp, splashed through the stream, and came bounding into my outstretched arms!

Sawyer

When I felt the tug on my leash, I almost shit my fur, literally. Well, that was a short-lived run for freedom. I looked up to see a guy holding my leash and something about him was familiar.

"What do we have here?" the guy said. At first, the sun was shining behind his head and it was hard to make him out. Then he gently pulled me up from the stream bed onto the bank. As I followed him, a tree blocked the sun, and I could make him out clearer. Hey, this was one of the guys we ate breakfast with this morning! What was his name? Matt! Yeah, that was it. Also, there was the other guy, Chuck, standing a little back nearer the

62

shelter.

"Sawyer?" Matt asked. "What are you doing on the trail by yourself?" I would have been happy to regale him with the whole tale if only I could. "Where is your Dad?" Again, all I could do was arch my eyebrows a bit and look back down the trail.

"Maybe," Chuck chimed in, "he got loose." Well, that's partially correct, but it wasn't because I wanted to get loose.

"Let's chill here for a bit and see if his Dad comes along," Matt suggested.

At least they weren't complete strangers or, even worse, friends of Ranger Dick. After I indicated with a bit of tug back toward the stream, they let me drink until I had slaked my thirst. Then we went and sat on the edge of the shelter floor. I curled up on the floor to get a little rest after that run. Matt and Chuck sat with their legs dangling over the side discussing all the scenarios that could have possibly led to me showing up here unaccompanied. They weren't even close to the truth.

After a short rest, I heard someone coming down the trail. I picked it up first, and Matt was a little surprised when I stood up and jumped down out of the shelter. He quickly grabbed my leash and he and Chuck both stood up as they finally heard someone approaching. I was nervous. What if Ranger Dick had hurt Dad and now he was here to get me? I stared furiously at the bend in the trail, waiting to see who it would be. The person came around the bend and my heart leaped. It was Dad! I surged forward, ripping the leash out of Matt's hand. I splashed through the stream and rushed into Dad's outstretched arms! Never had I been so happy to see him! I covered his face in licks, which he happily accepted.

Dad

"Did he get away from you?" Matt asked me when my little reunion with Sawyer was done and we had all gone back over to the shelter. We were sitting at the picnic table in front and

Sawyer was stuck to my side.

"I wish that was all it was," I said. That's when I think they got their first good look at me and could see I was flushed and close to all-out panic.

"What's going on?" Chuck asked me.

"Remember Ranger Dick?" I asked.

"Uh oh," they both said in unison.

I told them the whole story from when Sawyer killed the deer until I had shown up at the shelter. As they listened, their eyes and mouths grew wider with every new detail. When I was finally done, they were looking at me like they had no idea what to say. "What was I supposed to do?" I asked them. "There was no way I was letting him take Sawyer to his death."

"I don't blame you a bit!" Chuck said. "I'm not sure I would have been able to take him, but my big boy over here could." He winked at Matt who gave him a thumbs up.

"Thanks," I said. "But now what the fuck am I going to do? They'll be after us soon."

"What you need to do is get the hell out of Shenandoah National Park," Matt said. "I'm not sure what kind of jurisdiction the rangers have outside the park, but I'm pretty sure it would be a lot harder for them to confiscate Sawyer outside its boundaries."

That made sense and I nodded my agreement as I pulled my phone out to look at the Guthooks App to find the closest road that would take us out of the park.

Chuck pointed to my phone and said, "You need to turn that thing off right now and take out the battery."

Of course! How could I be so stupid? They could easily track my cell phone as soon as they figure out who I was. They probably didn't know right at that moment, but Ranger Dick had inspected my permit the other day and even if he didn't remember after the wallop he took to the head, the copy of it was deposited in the box at the beginning of the park. It was only a matter of time before they figured out who I was and all my pertinent details, including my phone number. This also made me think about my wife and how they would probably contact her soon if they didn't already have Sawyer and me in custody. I quickly thought about calling her to warn her, but I could see on the screen I didn't have a signal in this valley where the shelter was located. I couldn't take the risk that they wouldn't be already tracking it by the time I got to a sufficient elevation in which to get a signal.

"Right," I said to Chuck. I turned the phone off, flipped it over, pulled the cover off the back, and fished the battery out. I tossed them into my electronics bag in my pack. "While I didn't exactly plan for this turn of events, I did come prepared for such an occasion." They both looked at me questioningly as I dug around in my pack and came out with a bundle of folded paper wrapped in rubber bands. I leafed through the papers and pulled out a map labeled:

MAP 11
APPALACHIAN TRAIL
and other trails in
SHENANDOAH NATIONAL PARK
South District

I had brought along paper maps as a backup to the Guthook's App and my trail guide, and until now I had never even taken them out of my pack. The trail guide was paper as well, but it mostly dealt with what was on the AT itself. These maps, however, covered a wide range of side trails and roads throughout the park. Spreading the map over the picnic table, we all studied it.

Chuck pointed to a spot on the map and said, "Looks like Simmons Gap fire road would be the closest exit to the park."

Matt said, "That would work. We are parked at the Pinefield Gap parking lot, just a short hike on the other side of the trail where you turn off to come to this hut. We could drive you up to the fire road and out of the park."

"I was wondering how you got here ahead of us," I said.

65

"Yeah, we were just going to do a section of the AT today and that's where we started from," Matt said.

I began thinking about how much I was dragging them into this situation. "Are you guys sure you want to get involved in this? As of right now, you have plausible deniability. If you go any further, you might get into trouble."

They both looked at each other and shrugged their shoulders. "I don't think we could live with ourselves if we didn't try to help prevent them from killing your dog. At least I know I couldn't," Chuck said.

At this, Sawyer looked up from where he was lying by my feet and gave what looked like a very wide smile.

"Me either," Matt agreed.

I couldn't help but get choked up a bit at this. I mean, we had only just met this morning and while we formed a quick bond that hikers do along the trail, this was still a lot to commit to what was basically a stranger and his dog. "OK, but can we get down that road in your car? You know how those fire roads are." Fire roads are only roads in the loosest sense of the word. They are barely a path wide enough to get down and get rough in some places.

"Not a problem," Chuck said. "We have a Jeep Wrangler."

"Ha!" I exclaimed. "So do we." I took another look at the map then noticed something. "We may have a problem though." They both looked at me expectantly. "That fire road runs right by the Simmons Gap Ranger Station." This took no further explanation.

"Well, hell," Matt said.

I studied the map again for a few more minutes then said, "I think it would be wise if we didn't go north past the station. We are going to have to head south. It's a little longer on the Skyline Drive, but if we can get down to Browns Gap, there is a road that will take us out of the park." It was aptly titled Browns Gap Road. We agreed this was our best shot. We would take the short hike back to the parking lot and then get the hell out of Dodge.

66

Sawyer

I listened as the guys talked about what had happened and what they planned to do. I understood most of it and I was really thankful to hear Chuck say what he did about not letting them kill me. That would be my preference as well. Chuck and Matt gathered their stuff and Dad hoisted his pack and buckled it on. Chuck had slid my pack off earlier and when Dad put it back on I gave no resistance. I'd be happy to wear that pack for the rest of my life if we could just get the hell out of this mess. Why did I have to kill that animal? I don't know why. I couldn't stop myself, my predator instinct had taken over.

Dad hooked me to the hiking leash, and we started our trek back up the side trail to the big trail. That's what I thought of it. Dad and others had a different name for it but it was the big trail for me. We all, as I heard them discuss earlier, had hoped to avoid encountering anyone before we got to Pinefield Gap where Matt and Chuck's jeep was parked. That would not be the case though. As we approached the crossing of the big trail we saw another hiker coming from the left. There was no avoiding him, and to turn back now would have looked suspicious. I guess Dad thought the same because he continued the few more feet to the intersection and waited a few seconds to greet the hiker.

"How's it going?" Dad asked the approaching hiker. He was a thru-hiker by evidence of his enormous pack and bushy beard.

"Doing OK," he replied. At this point I had been through enough thru-hiker meetings to know that what usually came next was the exchange of trail names, which as of now, we still didn't have, but this guy launched right into telling us about something we already knew. "A little while back, I passed a group of day hikers that found an unconscious ranger on the side of the trail. It looked like they had the situation in hand, so I went on since I have miles to make today."

I looked at Dad, wondering what he would say. "Really?" Dad

said, with fake surprise in his voice. "My dog and I didn't see anything when we came that way earlier. Of course we have been taking a good long break at the shelter here. Was he still unconscious when you saw him?"

The hiker looked at Dad a little quizzically, but said, "He was starting to stir when I left but he was still pretty out of it. I can tell you this though. He had a pretty good knot on the side of his head. Somebody hit him with something I am willing to bet. You might want to keep especially vigilant."

"We will," Dad said. "Thanks for the heads up. Were the day hikers able to get him some help, do you know?"

"One of them hiked with me to the top of the next mountain to get a signal. He was still on the phone when I started down the other side. I'm sure they got a hold of somebody for help. Well, I gotta get down to the shelter to get water, then back to it. Maybe I'll see ya down the trail."

"O.K." Dad replied. "Maybe we will."

I was thinking I hope we don't as I watched the hiker stroll down the side trail we had just come up.

"We've got to get the hell out of here," Dad said to Matt and Chuck.

They agreed. We crossed the big trail and continued up the smaller trail on the other side. In about ten minutes we came out at the gap parking lot. It really wasn't a parking lot, it was more of a small turnout with room for about four cars to park along the side. At the moment, the only car there was a blue and white jeep. Don't let people tell you dogs are color blind. That's bullshit. We see colors just like humans do. Don't know where they got it in their head that we don't. Surely no dog ever told them as much. Chuck got in and started up the jeep while Dad and Matt chunked all the gear inside. Dad turned to me and said, "Sawyer, up!" He had already unclicked my leash and he didn't have to tell me more than once. I jumped in the back of the jeep just like I had done a million times before on our own.

Chuck guided the jeep from the turnout and headed what I guess was south since that's what they had agreed on before.

Matt sat beside him in the front passenger seat. Dad was behind Matt in the backseat with his pack laid out next to him. I was bringing up the rear in the cargo area. We cruised around a few bends in the road and I calmed down, thinking this would turn out all right, when I felt the jeep rapidly decelerate and throw me up against the back of the seat in front of me. "Shit!" I heard Matt say.

When I regained my footing, I looked forward to see what was going on. I saw a line of cars in front of us and at the beginning of that line were two trucks with flashing lights on their roof. That was not good.

"Fuck, what are we going to do?" Chuck asked anyone that would listen. I looked at Dad, who was busy looking through the window, but not the front window. He was looking through his side window.

"We are going to have to try and turn around, then take our chances going north," Matt said.

Dad spoke up. "That's not going to work. They would be on us in seconds." Dad looped one arm through his pack and opened his door just enough to allow passage and slipped out.

"What are you doing?" Matt cried.

Dad didn't immediately answer him. What he did was to reach his hand back in, pull the lever that released his seat back so it folded up and opened a path to the cargo area. Grabbing my leash, he dragged me out with him. Then he spoke, "I can't let you guys get any more involved in this. Thanks for all the help you've given us." With that, he pushed the door closed and led us off to the side of the road.

As of yet, we were still the last car in line and no other one had pulled up. This was a lucky break as there was no one to witness us skulking off the side of the road to a small trail Dad had evidently spied through his window. *Good job, Dad! I didn't even see that with my eyes.* We ascended a small hill into tree coverage that took us out of the immediate view of the road. Here, Dad stopped to get his pack properly situated and then looked at me. "What a fine mess we've gotten ourselves into, huh boy?" I was about to bark an agreement but then thought better of it. I settled for a small huff instead.

Dad

I really had gotten lucky on where we had come to a stop on the Skyline Drive. I had spotted a small concrete post and what looked like a trailhead on the side of the road up a small hill. As Sawyer and I had made our hasty getaway, I glanced at the post marker. The trail was named One Mile Run and it said the park boundary was 3.5 miles away. Even in a hurry, I had time to think. Why wasn't it named Three Point Five Mile Run trail?

When we had gotten over the first hill and out of sight of the Skyline Drive, I paused, got my pack fastened properly, and made sure Sawyer's leash was squared away. "What a fine mess we've gotten ourselves into, huh boy?" I said to him. He looked at me and gave a small huff. I was grateful for the huff and not a full-on bark. He seemed to be getting the hang of this stealth hiking we were going to need to do. If we could only do it for 3.5 miles and get the hell out of the park, we would be in a much better situation. I didn't think all our problems would be over, but I felt a lot more confident I could protect him if I was out of Ranger Dick's domain.

The trail descended and we hiked on for about ten minutes, never seeing another soul. At this point I halted and fished out the paper map that was stored in my right hip belt pocket. The map showed a steep descent into a valley that mostly followed a stream called One Mile Run. Mystery of the trail name solved there. It also showed the trail exiting the park and eventually ending up on what looked like some back roads. That area was marked NO PUBLIC ACCESS but at this point I didn't care. We'd take our chances if we could get out of the park.

I stowed the map and we got back to hiking. The trail descended steeply and even though I still had my knee braces on, our quick pace made them protest. We arrived at One Mile Run stream, which was flowing pretty well for being the middle of summer. We had to cross it several times and once we stopped to top of our water supply. So far we encountered no other hikers on this trail, and I didn't think we would. It didn't seem like a well-traveled path. The further we went, the more the trail seemed to become overgrown. We had to carefully seek out the next blue-blaze to keep on track. Another half mile along, we came to a huge tree blown down over the trail.

We tried to go around it but the foliage on both sides of the trail was too dense. Our only choice was to climb over it. I took my pack off and hoisted it over the fallen tree. Then I clambered up and over while Sawyer tried to follow me. This didn't work so well. Sawyer kept slipping off the branches and could not get a good pawhold. I ended up having to climb back over and then half pull and half push his hairy golden butt over the tree where he came down pretty hard on the other side and rolled over. If I hadn't known better, I would've sworn he was going to bite me after the evil look he gave me. Once over the fallen tree, we geared back up and continued down. We hadn't been walking more than ten minutes when we came across another blow down. "Jesus Christ!" I exclaimed, probably a bit too loud for someone on the lam. I dropped my pack again, hooking Sawyer to it, and made my way to the top of this obstacle. When I reached a sufficient height to see over it, I didn't like the view that awaited me. I could see several more blow downs just beyond this one. Fallen tree lying upon fallen tree with their various branches forming a daunting barrier.

I slipped back down to where Sawyer was waiting for me with an expectant look on his face. "Looks like our luck has run out boy," I said and sat down at the side of the fallen tree, hanging my head in despair. So much for our quick escape from the park. If I had been alone, I might make it out through all that debris, but there was no way I could get Sawyer through it. I was sitting there wondering what to do when I felt wetness on my face. I looked up to see Sawyer who had just given me an *it's going to be all right* lick. I reached up and gave him a good behind the ears scratch. "Thanks, boy. I needed that." We were going to have to backtrack and figure something else out. What that was, I didn't know, but I noticed it was getting late and we needed to get a move on.

Sawyer

I was still a bit perturbed at Dad for practically throwing me off the top of a tree but when I saw him sit down and hang his head after climbing to the top of this new one in our path, my anger drifted away. He was trying to save my ass and I should be more grateful. I stretched my leash and came up next to him, giving him a quick lick to the side of the face. He thanked me and gave me some ear scratches, which besides a nice T-Bone with ample meat left on it, was about one of the most enjoyable things. We didn't have time for much of that though. We geared up and headed back the way we had come.

When we reached the blown down tree we had originally crossed I let out an exasperated huff. I wasn't looking forward to doing this again. While still difficult, it went a little smoother this time and I managed not to go head over tail. On the other side, it was a lot slower going as we were climbing up the steep grade we had come down earlier. I think Dad was trying to figure out what to do next and wasn't in any hurry to get back to the big road where there would be other people and maybe friends of Ranger Dick.

I picked up the sounds of something up the trail. I looked over to Dad, and he was just plodding along not noticing anything. As we moved, I could hear the sounds of people talking! This was not good. *Hey, Dad! There are people coming!* Of course he couldn't hear me and he kept walking, unaware we were going to run into somebody. Could be bad somebodies. I needed to do something. I stopped in my tracks and when the stretched length of the leash was played out, Dad felt the tug.

"Sawyer," Dad said. "Let's go!" He tugged on the leash and

pulled me a few steps forward, but I dug in and tried to hold my ground. "What is up with you?" He tugged on the leash even harder and dragged me along. I couldn't compete with the pressure he was putting on my harness, so I did something I rarely ever do, I let out a small whine. That's not something Dad hears often, and this took him aback. He stopped trying to pull me and asked, "Is something wrong?" *Hell yeah something is wrong! People are coming! Don't you hear that?* But I guess he didn't and looking around I figured out why. We were right near the stream, which was babbling and creating noise. My canine ears could pick up the impending visitors, but Dad's useless human ones couldn't.

I let out one more whine, and then tugged him to the non-stream side of the trail. He followed me until we got to the tree boundary and then paused. "Are you sure?" he asked me. I answered by trudging into the overgrowth between the trees and when the leash tightened, he followed me. We bushwhacked our way several hundred yards through the trees and we hunkered down, looking back in the direction we had come. As we quieted down I could hear the sounds of people moving and talking. Dad now heard them too and gave me a wink. We couldn't get a clear view of who was coming down the trail with all the overgrowth in the way but we could see swatches of color going by. Even with my super-canine hearing I couldn't make out what the people were saying. We had no idea whether they were friend or foe and from the look on Dad's face I didn't think he wanted to chance finding out.

We stayed down until they were out of earshot, and then stayed a few minutes more to be sure. When I judged it was safe, I gave Dad a look. He seemed to get what I was saying because he stood up. "Sawyer," he said in a hushed tone. "It's getting late and we need to find some place to wait out the night before we figure out what we are going to do next." He looked around and then sighed. "We can't risk going back on that trail. We are going to have to bushwhack a bit and find a place to set up camp. Lead us boy. You saved our asses, so I'll follow you. Find a place for us to camp."

Wow, I thought. This was an honor. It was also a lot of pressure, but I was up for it. I started leading us farther into the underbrush and trees. I relaxed and let my natural sense of direction take over. I tried to take us through the path of least resistance but it wasn't easy. They didn't call it bushwhacking for no reason. Problem was, it was mostly the bush that did the whacking of us. We went on this way for a while going up and down several tree-covered hills and after ascending one particularly steep upgrade we started heading down the other side. There, at the bottom, next to a rock wall was a nice flat spot. I looked at Dad and then back at the spot. "That'll work, bud," he said.

Dad

Sawyer led us right to a natural camping spot. It was a flat area that butted up against a rock wall. There was a lot of tree cover, but one thing bothered me. I didn't know if they would break out a helicopter to search for the likes of me and the killer golden retriever, but I was worried the tent might be easy to spot from the air when I saw something interesting. In the side of the rock wall was what looked like a small door. What the hell? Sawyer and I went over to inspect. It was a rusty grate and looked like an entrance. To what? A mine? Surely not. I broke out my headlamp and shown it through the grating. Sure as shit, it was a mine! I could see a passageway that went on into the darkness beyond the range of my lamp.

If we could get past this grate we could spend the night here and not have to worry about getting spotted from the air. I looked at the grate wondering how securely it was fastened to the wood frame that made up the door. I grabbed it and gave it a tug. The whole thing fell over and almost squashed Sawyer. Guess it wasn't all that secure. Sawyer gave me a bit of a side-eye glance at that close call. "Sorry, buddy," I told him. "However, unless there is a bear, orc, or Balrog in there, this is where we are going to spend the night." He gave me a bit of an uncertain stare and I didn't blame him. This felt like the Fellowship of the Ring entering the Mines of Moria, and if you read the book or saw the movie, you know how that turned out. If you didn't, let me assure you, it was less than an ideal situation for the Fellowship. I hoped it wouldn't be the same for this one.

I grabbed my pack, which I had earlier dropped, and led the way into the mine entrance. Sawyer didn't look all that enthusiastic about this impromptu spelunking trip, but he came in with me, and after unhooking him from the leash, explored his surroundings. In the headlamp's light, I could see it was mostly flat in here. There looked like there was a place where there might have been mine cart tracks at one time, but they were long gone. Sawyer headed back further in the mine and I yelled at him to come back. I had no idea what was back there. I was sure, at some point, a mine will drop and it could be straight down. I didn't want Sawyer to survive Ranger Dick and then bite it plummeting to the bottom of a mine shaft.

I hadn't need worry though. As I got to the back of the mine to retrieve Sawyer, I saw another metal grate affixed across the path that led to just what I had been worried about. There *was* a shaft and God knows if the grate hadn't been there, Sawyer might have had a one-way ticket to the bottom. I tested this grate by shaking it and was glad to find it was firmly in place. I guess being out of the weather; it had fared better. "Better be more careful home boy," I told Sawyer.

The foyer to the mine, which is how I thought of it because it looked like a transitional room from the outside to the underbelly of the mine, was damp but that couldn't be helped. I sat about unpacking some stuff from my pack and that's when I heard a loud grumble! Not from a bear or other creature that had taken up residence. It was actually my stomach. I realized that in all the excitement today, we hadn't had a single thing to eat since that wonderful breakfast Matt and Chuck had provided us that morning. I was ravenous and I am sure Sawyer was too.

However, it was going to be a cold meal tonight. I didn't know if my little stove could cause enough carbon dioxide to build up in the foyer, but I wouldn't take the chance. Besides, having an open flame showing when you were being hunted probably wasn't the best idea. So it would be some sausage, tortillas, and dog food on the menu tonight. I passed on the dog food though.

As I was rummaging around in my pack to get the food bag I saw Ranger Dick's radio. I had forgotten all about it! I put all thoughts of food on hold as I grabbed the radio and turned it on. I saw on the display that the battery level was 82%. Static was the only thing coming from the radio at the moment. I found the volume control and turned it down a bit so as not to attract anyone's attention that might be in the area. There was a button on the radio labeled *scan* and I pushed it. The display started cycling through frequencies and not long after, it locked on to one.

"Party three report your position," I heard. "This is party three. We are set up at Browns Gap Road. No signs of any hikers trying to exit the park via this route."

Shit! This did not sound good. I listened some more and heard other reports. It was all the same story. They were blocking off any exit from the park. Thanks to some blown down trees, we missed our opportunity to get out. Now we were in big fucking trouble. I couldn't think about it anymore. I was hungry and exhausted. I'm sure Sawyer was the same. I turned off the radio to conserve the battery. We had our meager dinner, then I broke out my sleeping bag and pad and set it all up the best I could. That's when I also discovered something in my pack I had forgotten about. It was the tall boy Bud Lite beer that I had bought at the camp store that morning. I remember thinking then I would rest at a peaceful campsite when I popped that bad-boy open. I didn't think I would be in a mine the next time I held it in my hand. I placed the beer on the floor, thinking it wasn't a good idea to be drinking now.

Before I crawled in to my sleeping bag I went back out to the entrance to the mine and picked up the fallen grate. I leaned it back up against the door frame so it would form somewhat of a barrier against any unwanted visitors, at least the four legged variety. There was nothing I could do if the two legged variety came calling. I tried to put it out of my mind as Sawyer and I settled down to get some sleep. I figured tomorrow was going to have its share of adventure and we needed to be rested for it. Then I said, "Fuck it!" to no one in particular and grabbed the beer. I popped the top and drank it all down in about three swigs. This calmed me down somewhat, and I fell asleep.

Sawyer

I watched Dad from the spot where I had laid down. After he downed his beer (man he chugged that thing) he was asleep in no time. As tired as I was, I wasn't quite ready to drift off yet. I thought about him calling me out earlier about the mine shaft. I know he was trying to look out for me, but it's not like I was going to jump into the thing. Give me some credit. As I lay there, I thought about the events of the day. I know I had gotten us in to some major trouble but I couldn't dwell on that fact anymore. What was done was done. I had to think about the way forward. I needed to get smarter about not following all my base instincts and instead, make moves based on our survival. I had to step up and become a partner to Dad. As I was thinking about all the ways I could do this I finally drifted off.

I woke up a few times in the night, alerted by sounds I heard outside. I checked my impulse to bark at any of the noises and just continued to listen until I was sure they were all natural sounds and not a danger. I don't think Dad woke up once. That's all right. I could handle the watch at night. When the grate covering the door became visible in the growing morning light, Dad woke up. He set about fixing us some cold breakfast and he packed up all our stuff.

Dad got down on his knees and looked at me eye to eye. "Sawyer," he said. "I'm not sure yet what we are going to do but

I need you to understand something. We may have to hurry to avoid coming into contact with people that don't have our best interest in mind. In order to do that, I'm not going to leash you up today. But I need you to stay with me and not run off? Do you understand?"

I understood but saw Dad put his head in his hands, "I wish I knew if this was getting through to you."

It is getting through to me, Dad! I have already decided I have to ignore my silly instincts and do my part to get us out of this thing. He couldn't hear that, so I just reached over and gave him a lick on the face.

Dad smiled and said, "I'll take that as a sign you understand. Now I have to think about a plan for getting us out of this mess."

Dad pulled out his map and studied it for what seemed like an eternity. Then he clicked on that box with voices. He listened for a bit and then clicked it back off. "While they are blocking off all exits from the park, it sounds like they are concentrating most of the search effort in the southern district," he said out loud. I wasn't sure if he was talking to me or just making a statement, so I didn't react. "We need to go north for now to get out of this area, then we'll figure out the next step."

We exited the mine and true to his word, Dad did not put the hiking leash on me. I stayed close by and we started hiking in the same direction I had led us last night. The going was tough. The trees and underbrush were thick. We were on a downslope and we both had trouble keeping our feet. We were like tennis balls bouncing off the trees and getting stuck in the brush. We continued this way for some time until we came to a small flowing river again.

We were beat, tired, dirty, and scratched up from the hike thus far. I was also thirsty and drank from the river. Dad grabbed my harness and drew me back. "No boy, I know I've let you drink straight from water sources in the past, but now we can't take the chance. We need to filter before we drink. You could get sick and that's the last thing we need right now." I understood this but I had to fight my instinct to sate my thirst.

I waited until Dad filled one of his water bottles from the river, attached the filter thing on it, and squeezed out some water straight into my collapsible water bowl that Dad withdrew from my pack. I gulped it all up. Dad filled up another bottle, put the filter on, and drank straight from it. After that he refilled all our water bottles, and we set off again.

This time we started going uphill, and if I thought the previous hike was difficult, I would have done it twice before doing this one. The climbing was very tough through the mess of flora in the area. We both slipped continuously as we tried to fight our way up to the next tree. For every step we took forward it felt like we slid two steps back. Eventually we leveled off and I noticed the trees thinning. At this point Dad stopped and told me to sit and wait. He went ahead a bit and disappeared from sight. I didn't want to wait, and I wasn't tied to anything to make me wait, but I had promised Dad I would behave, so I did. A short while later, Dad came back in view and told me to follow him. I happily complied.

We came to a clearing in the woods. It looked like some kind of rough path but with two trails running side by side. I think this is what Dad called a fire road. Dad turned to me and said, "I didn't see anybody when I looked before, but now it's your turn. Tell me if you hear something boy." Finally a chance to help out. I cocked my head to one side and then to the other. I heard nothing in the immediate area. I heard what I thought might be traffic down the path to our right, but it seemed to move past this road. "You hear anything?" Dad asked me. I wasn't sure how to communicate that I thought we were good to go, so I trotted out into the middle of the road and turned around in a circle, hoping he would get the message. "Guess that means we're good to go," he said. *Right on target! Good job, Dad!*

We turned right on the road and started down it slowly, keeping to the left side of it. I'm guessing that was so we could quickly take cover if someone were to come. As we made our way down the road in this fashion, we got closer to the sounds of occasional traffic and it worried me. I hated doing this, but

LEE LOVELACE

I saw no choice. I stopped and whined at Dad. Dad looked at me and said, "I think I know what you're worried about. Don't be. I know there are going to be cars where we are going. Trust me, I have a plan." I thought that phrase had been uttered at the beginning of a lot of plans gone awry, but I didn't have a plan so I went with it. Not long after, I started getting glimpses of a big road through the trees to our left. I could see cars pass on it from time to time. Then Dad stopped us short and we stepped into the cover of the trees again. Just ahead, the fire road intersected another trail and from the white stripe I could see on a tree down there, I knew it was the big trail, beyond that, the big road.

CHAPTER EIGHT

Expect The Unexpected

Dad

Trust me, I have a plan I said to Sawyer. Hell, I didn't know if I trusted the plan. It was risky but I thought we had a shot. We had spent the better part of the morning bushwhacking north. We had passed Two-mile Run River (they did some creative naming of rivers here) and then a difficult climb to the Beldor fire road. A turn left to the west, and a few miles hike on that road would have led out of the park. That was no good, however, since I had already heard on the radio that the exit was blocked. So we had turned right and headed east back toward the AT and Skyline Drive. We hunched down in the cover of some trees just off the fire road. Ahead, we could see the intersection of the fire road, the AT, and Skyline Drive. The AT crosses Skyline drive here and continues on the other side. Also on the other side is a minor road that leads to the Simmons Gap Ranger Station. Yup! The same station we had wanted to avoid yesterday. This was the plan. Go to the place they least expected us to be. The way I figured, if everyone was out blocking off exits and looking for us, there couldn't be many rangers at the station. It would take some stealth and a lot of luck, but if we could find a place to hole up near there for now, we could come up with the next step in our exit strategy without having to worry about keeping on the move. I really hoped this was as clever as I thought it was. Otherwise, things would not go well for me.

81

They would go even worse for Sawyer.

For this next move, I hooked Sawyer back to the hiking leash. I couldn't afford for us to get separated right now. I watched the intersection and when I was sure there were no hikers coming on the trail and no cars on the road; we bolted! Sawyer ran right along with me as we crossed the road unseen and got to the other side. We were still not out of the woods yet. Out of the woods, ha! We had to make it a little ways down the road to the ranger station. I had been to the ranger station once a few years ago when my wife and I had been driving down the Skyline. We had just pulled in to see what it looked like. If I remembered right, there were several old abandoned buildings from a different configuration long ago. I hoped they were still there.

We ran along looking for vehicles or people, ready to duck into the woods at the side of the dirt road if either one were to approach. As luck would have it, we made it to the station without encountering either. I relaxed some when I saw the old buildings were still there. One of them looked like an old shack, but I think it used to be the ranger station back in the day. The current ranger station was a much bigger stone house just down the hill from the shack. At that station, I could see one green and white truck with U.S. PARK RANGER written on the side. So probably one or two rangers there at home base, like I thought.

We made our way over to the shack. There was a rusty hasp on the door that looked like it had once had a padlock, but there was no lock in evidence now. There was a window next to the door and next to that was an old dilapidated sign that I could still barely make out. It said **DAYS SINCE LAST ACCIDENT** and next to it was a spot for hanging a little number tile. The space was vacant. I couldn't help but think that Ranger Dick might want to update this to say **DAYS SINCE LAST INCIDENT** and hang a little **1** tile next to it. I looked through the window and saw nothing that would prevent our entry, so I pushed on the door and it reluctantly squeaked open. I took no more time to survey, I tugged Sawyer with me and we entered the shack and shut the door.

Through the light coming in the window I could see there wasn't much in here but dust and spider webs. There were some old pieces of lumber in a corner that might have been used in a park project at one time. It was a bit creepy and had a long abandoned feeling to it. I dropped my pack, unleashed Sawyer, grabbed one piece of lumber, dragged it over and placed it in front of the inward swinging door to prevent anyone from coming in. I also noticed something odd. There was one of those old timey blinds rolled up above the window. You know the kind that you slowly pulled down and it locked, but you yank on it and it rolls up? I remembered as a kid how those things didn't always work and would jerk right out of your hand as it quickly rolled back up, maybe taking a chunk of your nose with it. I reached up and slowly pulled on the blind. It unwound with no problem, and when I had extended it to cover the whole window, I released it. My nose was safe. The blind stayed down and now we were protected from prying eyes. We were also mostly in the dark, so I had to break out my headlamp to see.

It was after noon hour so I gave Sawyer some dog food and I ate a pepperoni and cheese tortilla wrap. After that, I had intended to break out the map and figure out our next move but I was dog tired. I wondered if Sawyer ever thought he was human tired. See, these are the kinds of things I thought about when exhausted. All the bushwhacking had done a number on me. I laid my head back on my pack, intending to just chill, and before I knew it, I was asleep.

Sawyer

Just as I was finishing up my lunch I saw Dad pull out his sleeping pad, lay down, and prop his head on his pack. In no time, he was snoring. I hope nobody heard it because, man, he could saw some logs. I was pretty beat myself so I laid down, splaying my back legs to the side. Mom and Dad always said I was doing the flounder booty when I lay like this. I had no idea what that meant, but it was comfortable to me. So as I lay flounder booty style, I also closed my eyes, but I kept my ears open.

Sometime later, I heard what sounded like a car approaching up the dirt road. Glancing over at Dad, I saw that he was still snoozing, and wondered whether to wake him. Nah, let him sleep for now. If things got dangerous, I'd alert him. The car came closer, and then stopped. I heard two doors open and close and could hear some voices. Then, with my super nose, I detected the smell of smoke. Not like a forest fire, but something else. I knew this smell from a while ago. Oh yeah, it was the smell of a cigarette. Mom used to smoke, but she had since kicked the habit. Now I used my super hearing (damn, I am one super dog) to listen to what the two smokers were saying.

"I think the guy and his dog got out before we clamped down," said a male sounding voice.

"Could be," said a female sounding voice. "We are probably just wasting our time."

"Something still sounds off about Russell's story. Why would a hiker attack him for no reason?"

"He said the guy must have been scared about getting in trouble for the dead deer."

"That doesn't make any sense. The guy called it in to the station himself. Why wouldn't he just hike on if he thought he was going to get in trouble?"

"Good point. You know Russell, always bullying hikers. I wouldn't be surprised if he didn't say some bullshit that incited the whole incident."

"Yeah, neither would I. Well, we better go check in and have some lunch before we head back out on Russell's goose chase."

I could hear, what I now assumed were rangers, get back in their car and drive down the hill. So, if I had this right, Russell, must be Ranger Dick and he'd fed everyone a line of bullshit about what had really happened. The whole thing about putting me down was probably just him being, well, a dick. The other rangers seemed cool but I'm sure they had no choice but to pursue us when told a story like that. That, and Dad *did* whack him upside the head with his stick. I wish Dad had been awake to hear this. All the trouble we were in due to this guy Russell. Russell my furry ass, he'll always be Ranger Dick to us.

After this bit of excitement, I drifted off to sleep myself. I woke some time later when I heard Dad stirring. "Damn! I didn't mean to sleep this long, Sawyer," he said as he was picking himself up off the floor. Dad carefully pulled back the thing covering the window and peeked outside. I caught a glimpse and I could see that the light was already starting to grow weak. *So what's the plan Dad?*

As if he heard me he turned and said, "We have to figure out a plan." *You figure it out. I'll follow.* "I know we need to get north where maybe the search is a little less concentrated. Then maybe we can slip out somehow." *Sounds good. How we gonna do that without getting caught?* "Let me look at the map." *OK.*

Dad pulled out the map and studied it. After a bit, he folded it back up and put it away. "Our best shot at getting north is going to be on the AT. I know it sounds crazy, but there aren't any other side trails around here that will take us that way." It sounded like he was trying to convince himself more than he was talking to me. "I'm tempted to try night hiking, but I'm too worried that a headlamp bobbing around in the dark would attract too much attention. We are just going to have to be careful as we go. Right boy?" *Uhm, yeah. Sure.* "I'll be the eyes and you'll be my nose and ears. You can warn me when someone is coming, OK?" *Sure thing! Although it seems like I get two senses and you only have to do one, but hell, I'm up for it.* I tried to show my acceptance of the mission by doing a little huff. Dad seemed to get the message and gave me a good ear scratch.

I heard vehicles approaching again. I got up and cocked my ear to the door. Dad got that message too and peaked outside the window. Several vehicles approached and kept going down the hill to the ranger station. He seemed satisfied when nobody approached our hiding spot. Dad settled back into the room and reached up to fiddle with the light on his head. The white light went out and in its place a red light now shown. Dad addressed my quizzical look. "It's going to be dark soon and I don't want the white light to cause any shadows on the window blind. We'll have to get by with the red light." The red light cast an eerie glow about the room but it was enough to see by.

"I've had enough of cold food. I think we can risk lighting the camping stove since the integrated pot will cover up most of the flame. I'll even share some with you. How about some lasagna tonight?" *Works for me!* "Good thing we resupplied yesterday morning. We still have enough food for about four days."

Dad set about making the lasagna and, boy, was it good. We heard a few more vehicles coming and leaving, but then things settled down and got quiet. We risked a little sojourn outside the shack to relieve ourselves, then settled in for the night. Throughout the night, I slept with one ear and one nostril open.

Dad

My alarm went off at 5:00 AM. I wanted to get up and out before things got too busy around here. I peeked out the window and could just see the glowing of the coming dawn lighting the sky. We packed up and prepared to head out. No breakfast right now. We could munch on something on the trail.

"All right," I said to Sawyer. "No leash today either. You ready to be my nose and ears?" He looked at me as if to say *let's get this show on the road.* "You got it, boy. Let's go."

I slid the piece of lumber out of the way and cracked the door enough to survey the surroundings. There was nobody about, so we scurried out. We made it back down the dirt road and without hesitation, Sawyer took a right and headed north on the trail. He stayed in front of me as we made our way. The trail ascended but not too steeply and by the time we made it to the top of the rise, the sun had fully risen. We were going to have to be on guard. I half hoped it would rain. That would have helped with keeping some hikers off the trail and cutting visibility. I had no idea what the weather was supposed to be since I had to ditch my phone. Speaking of things that were no longer useful. I had tried the radio before we left this morning and couldn't pick up anything. I think they just now realized I had taken Ranger Dick's radio and were now staying off the air in case I was listening in. I still had the radio in my pack, but now it was dead weight.

I produced a pack of strawberry frosted Pop Tarts from one of my hip belt pockets, and Sawyer and I munched on them for breakfast as we continued on the trail. We descended a bit and had still not encountered anyone when the trail crossed the Skyline Drive. We stopped just inside the tree cover before proceeding across the road. "Are we good, boy?" I asked Sawyer. He looked at me and didn't make any demonstrable gestures so I took that as an all-clear response. I was a little nervous crossing the road without him on a leash but I was going to have to trust him. I waited longer to make sure there were no cars and then said, "Now!" We both scurried across the road and into the tree cover on the other side. Sawyer did great getting across the road, so I reached down and gave him a congratulatory pat on the head.

Our first bit of excitement came about fifteen minutes later. Sawyer was ahead of me a little way when he stopped. I caught up to him and saw him cock his head back the way we had come. He listened for a few seconds, and then gave me a loud huff. That was all I needed. We both shuffled into the trees on the side of the trail and hunkered down. Just a few seconds later I could hear the sounds of someone coming up the trail and not too long after that I saw them. It was a girl, and by the looks of her big pack and the items hanging off of it, she was a thru-hiker. She was tall, blond, and looked like she was in her early 30s. She was moving along at quite a pace and I could see she was listening to something on her phone. She had one ear bud in her left ear and the other dangled over her right shoulder. This was the recommended way of listening to music, audio books, or podcasts while hiking. You keep one ear bud out so you can still hear the sounds of the trail. Like people approaching, or more importantly, the staccato sound of a rattlesnake shaking its tail in warning. Even though she was wearing the ear buds in this configuration it probably still served our purpose as she seemed intent on what she was listening to and passed us by without notice.

We resumed our hike and in the next several hours we had to cross the Skyline Drive one more time without incident. However, we encountered two more hikers we had to take cover from. These hikers were SOBO, and in each case Sawyer alerted me ahead of time and we had no problem hiding from them.

While hiking, I reached for the water bottle attached to the strap of my pack and noticed it had only a swallow left. I knew my other water bottle was already empty. I called Sawyer over and looked inside his pack. There was only a bit left in one of his two bottles. In our hurry to get out of the old ranger shack this morning I had neglected to fill our water bottles from a spigot on the other side of the shack. What a rookie mistake.

The paper map didn't show water sources like the Guthooks app had, other than major creeks or rivers. I was going to have to keep a lookout for a source. If we didn't find one soon, we would get awfully thirsty. We ascended again and a little while later we came to an intersection of a blue-blazed trail. It was the trail to the High Top hut. I knew from experience that there was usually a water source near a hut. That would solve our water problem, but it presented another one. It was around midday and hikers liked to converge on the huts to eat lunch and refill their water. I didn't see any other choice. We would just have to be careful and hope for the best.

"Sawyer, we have to go to the hut to get water. I need you to be vigilant," I told him. Why did I use the word *vigilant* when talking to a dog? Why did I use *any* words with a dog? I don't know but I often felt like he understood me perfectly. Just maybe not when I used words like *vigilant*.

He looked at me like he understood, so we proceeded up the blue-blazed trail. It was only about 0.1 mile, and when we crept up to the hut I didn't see anyone. Sawyer looked around for a second and gave me a little huff. I wasn't sure what the huff was for, because as far as I could tell we were alone. There was a sign saying WATER and pointing to a trail just before the hut so we set off that way. About another 0.1 mile and we came to a piped spring. I grabbed my Smart Water bottle, removed the filter from the top, and filled it up from the spring. After screwing the filter back on to the top, I upended the bottle and chugged until the whole bottle was gone. This is what hikers called cameling up. Drinking as much water as you can before topping off your bottles for later consumption. Sawyer had no hump, other than his pack, but he wanted to camel up too. I removed his water dish from his pack and poured him a whole dish of filtered water from a second round at the spring. By the time we were done, we had drunk more than our fill, and were now sporting full water bottles.

We made our way back up the trail, and as we neared the hut again I paused. My stomach grumbled and I was thinking this would be a good time and place to have lunch. Then I thought again. This would *not* be a good place to have lunch. Better we eat off the trail somewhere, so as not to be caught with full mouths by other hikers or rangers. Just as I was finishing up this thought I saw the door to the privy across from the other side of the hut bang open and the same girl hiker we had seen passing us earlier, stepped out. Sawyer and I both froze, not sure what to do. The girl took a few steps toward the hut before she noticed us standing there with our shocked expressions. "Oh, my gawd!" she exclaimed. "Y'all are the ones they're looking for!"

Sawyer

I tried to tell Dad earlier that something was fishy about this hut, and by fishy I meant I smelled some strong orders of fish around here, but when he headed down the other trail, I thought he meant to bypass the hut and didn't think more of it. Especially when we got to the water, because I was thirsty as hell! Now here we stood, busted.

That's when my sixth sense kicked in. I instinctively knew this girl was good and would not be a problem for us. I trotted over to where she was standing. "Sawyer, no!" Dad hissed. I ignored him and continued on. I walked right up to the girl and nuzzled her thigh. There are few people that can resist the thigh nuzzle of a Golden Retriever, and this girl was no exception.

"Aww," she said in what Dad calls a southern drawl. She reached down and gave my head a thorough rubbing.

"Sorry," Dad said to her. "He's a friendly fur face."

"No problem at all. I love dogs. Y'all *are* the ones they are looking for, ain't ya?"

Dad sighed warily and then reluctantly said, "Yeah, I guess we are. What have you heard?"

"Well, from the rangers I heard you attacked one of them for no reason."

"That's bullshit."

"Yeah, I know. Last night I stayed at Pinefield Hut. A couple of guys came in and told us you only attacked the ranger when he tried to take your dog after saying he was going to basically kill him."

"That must have been Matt and Chuck. They tried to help us out."

"Yeah, it was them. They told everyone there the whole story. They wanted us to spread the word up and down the trail grapevine that what the rangers are saying is a lie."

Well, the other rangers were lied to also, as I now knew from overhearing the smokers conversation yesterday, but there was no way for me to tell them that.

"Don't worry," she said to Dad. "I'm not telling them anything. My trail name is Southern Comfort, by the way. I'm sure you can tell by my Alabama accent why I got this trail name, even though I don't like whiskey."

"We don't have trail names, but my real name is…"

"Sure you do!" Southern Comfort said as she cut Dad off. She pointed to him. "Your trail name is MoMo." She then grabbed my face and squished it between her hands. "And this cutie patootie is Rush!"

Dad gave her a weird look. I gave her one too but only because she still had my face squished up. "What are you talking about?" Dad asked her.

"Look at the shelter log." She pointed to the hut.

Dad walked over to the hut, hopped up, and grabbed the shelter log. I extracted my face from Southern Comfort's hands and walked over to the open end of the hut. Dad was reading the log and I noticed something next to him. It was a pack. It must be her pack. It was leaning against the closest wall to the trail. That's why we hadn't noticed it when we first came by the hut. She must have been having lunch here and was in the privy when we passed. I took a quick sniff and could detect the smell of the fish coming from her pack. That must have been her lunch.

Dad finished his reading and then said to Southern Comfort, "I don't understand. Why did we get trail names and why are people talking about us in the shelter logs?"

"Last night the hikers at the Pinefield hut bestowed trail names on you two so we could pass word around about you without the rangers knowing who we are talking about. Since you have never had trail names they wouldn't know."

Wow, I had a trail name now! I wondered what it meant.

Dad said, "That is amazing! Every hiker felt this way?"

"Everyone that was there last night did. I can't imagine a hiker that wouldn't sympathize with your situation. Maybe a day hiker that doesn't know what's going on, but surely not a thru or section hiker."

"So how did you come up with the trail names? I think I know where Sawyer's came from. Rush's song, Tom Sawyer?"

Who is Rush and what is this song he was talking about?

"Yeah that's it," Southern Comfort said. "That, and the fact that we hear he can really rush along the trail when he has to."

Well, that's true, but I'm going to have to get Dad to play me

LEE LOVELACE

this song so I can see if I like it.

"Alright, but I have no clue where mine came from. What the hell is MoMo?"

She gave a little chuckle. "Do you watch *The Walking Dead*?"

Oh, I knew the answer to that one. I had often laid on the couch or bed next to Dad and Mom when they watched the zombie show.

"I do, actually," Dad replied. "But what does that have to do with..." He stopped speaking and looked up at the top of the trees for a few seconds. "Morgan?" he asked.

"Yeah. He moved over to the spin off *Fear The Walking Dead* before he got that nickname. You remember?"

Oh! I knew this one too! The guy on the show, Morgan, walked around with a stick and beat the hell out of zombies and other people with it. One of the other characters on the show gave him the nickname MoMo.

"I do," Dad said. "MoMo and Rush huh? Clever."

"We all thought so too," she said as she reached over and tapped Dad's walking stick.

They talked a little more as I laid down by the picnic table outside the hut to take a rest. As they talked about the usual hiker things like it was an ordinary day on the trail, I started to drift off to sleep when I heard something that caught my attention. What was that? It sounded like, no, it couldn't be, it sounded like a car. A car out here on the trail? *Dad! A car is coming!* Oh shit, that won't work. I gave a loud huff and when that didn't get my point across, I did it again.

Momo

"Shit!" I yelled.

"What?" Southern Comfort asked.

"Someone is coming."

"How do you know that? I don't hear anything."

"Sawyer, or should I say Rush, does. The huffing is his signal to me."

"Really?"

"Yes, really."

"Maybe it's just another hiker?"

I looked at Sawyer and said, "Is it a person coming?"

Sawyer looked at me and huffed heavily again.

"I don't think so."

"You couldn't possibly know that."

"We have a way of communicating. I can't explain right now. We probably don't have long." As I finished that prophetic statement, we heard the distant sound of a vehicle approaching. There was an overgrown path next to the hut that might have been a road at one time, but what now looked like nothing more than a horse trail. The sound of the vehicle got louder and there was no mistaking its destination. I started looking around in panic, wondering what to do.

"The bear box!" Southern Comfort said.

"What? You mean get in it?"

"Yeah, you don't have time for anything else. I'll act like I'm here alone. Now go!"

I didn't like the idea of us being cornered in the bear box, but she was right. I had no time to put on my pack and head into the woods. Whoever was coming would surely be on us by then. I grabbed my pack and told Sawyer to follow me as I headed over to the bear box. I opened it up, threw my pack in and slid into the cramped space. There was just enough room for Sawyer to join me but it would be tight.

That wouldn't be a problem, however, as Sawyer refused to come into the box. "Get in!" I hissed at him in a low voice. He looked at me in the box, then back to the sound of the approaching vehicle, then back to me again. He gave me one low huff and took off into the woods almost faster than I could follow. Rush, indeed.

I couldn't worry about it anymore, as I could now clearly hear a vehicle laboring up the path. Southern Comfort heard it too, shrugged her shoulders before she closed the door to the

93

LEE LOVELACE

bear box with me inside. I could hear her scrambling around outside as the vehicle noise got louder, then stopped. A car door slammed and then someone was speaking. "Hello ma'am. Are you alone here?" I knew the voice at once. It was Ranger Dick! Great! Of all the rangers, it had to be him. This guy kept turning up like a bad penny.

"Yes, I am," I heard her say.

"Are you thru hiking?"

"Yes."

"Have you seen a man on the trail hiking with a Golden Retriever?"

"No, but I wish I had. I love dogs."

"You wouldn't like this dog," I heard Ranger Dick say gruffly. "He's a dangerous animal and his owner attacked me a couple of days ago."

"Really?" I heard her say in feigned surprise. "You wouldn't think a Golden Retriever would be dangerous? And why would his owner attack you for no reason?"

There was silence for a moment as I conjured up an image of Ranger Dick's face contorting with anger at this thru-hiker challenging his authority. I clamped a hand over my mouth to stop from laughing. That would not do at all.

"I didn't say he attacked me for no reason. Let me see your permit," I heard him demand.

"Sure. It's right here." I heard her shuffle around with her pack.

There was another lull in the conversation as I heard him crinkling the permit paper. "This thing is barely legible."

"Yeah, it got wet when I was crossing a stream the other day. I have to have it on the outside of my pack so I couldn't avoid it."

"What's your trail name?"

"Southern Comfort. I'm from the south, so ya know? Don't like whiskey though."

I heard him grumble something inaudible and he walked around the hut site. I heard the privy door open and close. Then his footsteps were very loud as he came near the bear box. Shit!

94

Was he going to look in here? The handle to the door turned and a sliver of daylight appeared... Fuck! But before the door opened enough to get a clear view, there was a loud crash from the woods on the other side of the hut!

"What was that?" I heard Southern Comfort yell.

The line of daylight disappeared, as Ranger Dick let go of the bear box door and rushed over to investigate the sound. I put my hand up to stop the door from completely closing. No way could I stay here any longer. He would surely come back to finish his exploration of the box before he was done. I pushed the door open enough for me to get a look outside. I didn't see Ranger Dick or Southern Comfort, but by the sound of it, they were moving around on the other side of the hut looking for the source of the crashing sound. I grabbed my pack, slipped out of the bear box, and eased the door shut. I scurried over to the privy and slipped inside. My new hiding place wasn't any better than my old one, especially since it was a hole in the ground filled with piss and shit, but Ranger Dick had already searched it, so it was my best shot.

After a few minutes, they came back from the other side of the hut. I could see through a slit between the boards of the privy. "That was a pretty big widow maker that fell," I heard Southern Comfort say. "Good thing it didn't hit the shelter." Widow makers were dead trees or limbs. Hikers avoided them when pitching a tent or hammock because they can fall and make your significant other a widow, or widower; let's keep it equal opportunity here folks.

"Yeah," Ranger Dick said. I could get a good look at him now and I could see that his right wrist was wrapped in a bandage where I had whacked him with my stick. The side of his face was also bruised where he had taken a wallop. Wait a minute. Where *was* my stick? I didn't have it! Did I leave it in the bear box?

I saw Ranger Dick return to the bear box and grab the handle. Fuck me running! He would not forget the sight of that stick anytime soon. One look at it and he would know I was around. He turned the handle and opened the bear box. I held my breath for what seemed like an eternity before I saw him close the box and return to the hut. Oh, my God! I guess I didn't leave it in there either. Where was it? Last time I remember seeing it was when it was leaning on the wall inside the hut.

"When you get to Swift Run Gap in a few miles get a new permit from the park entrance station," Ranger Dick ordered her.

"Sure thang," she replied.

"You should know, I have the authority to kick you out of the park if you don't have a valid permit."

"Won't be a problem."

With that, Ranger Dick got back in his green and white park truck, cranked it up, and headed back down the path. As much as I wanted to get out of that stinky privy, I waited a few more minutes to make sure he would not double back for any reason. It looked like Southern Comfort was doing the same but she eventually got up and went over to the bear box. She opened it. "Where the fuck are you?" she said, throwing her hands up.

I laughed and exited the privy. "Same place you surprised us from!" I said as she looked at me with an incredulous expression.

"Well played!" she said and laughed.

I made my way over to the hut and looked inside. Nothing! "You looking for this?" she asked. I turned around and saw her stooped in front of the hut dragging out something from the foot of space underneath it. It was my walking stick. "I saw it after you got in the bear box and barely had time to shove it under there before he got here.

I laughed again. "Well played to you also! Not only that, but for whatever you did to distract him from the bear box."

"Oh, I can't take credit for that one. We just got lucky."

"So an actual widow maker came down just at the moment I needed a distraction?"

"Yeah, can you believe that? I thought we were screwed for sure. Man that guy is a dick."

"Oh, not only is he a dick, he is *the* dick. That's the guy who tried to take Sawyer. We call him Ranger Dick."

"A well-deserved name. So what happened with Rush there?"

"I guess he didn't want to be in the bear box. I need to go find him." I grabbed my walking stick and tried to decide which way to go when I heard noises moving in the woods beyond the hut. My first thought was that Ranger Dick parked his truck down the path and walked back up to try and catch us. But when a golden furry face appeared from around the hut wall I relaxed. Sawyer was back.

"Rush!" Southern Comfort said.

"Come here, bub!" I said and held out my arms.

He came running right into the arms of Southern Comfort. That was one woman loving dog there. I eventually got my turn and did a combination pat down and inspection. He looked none the worse for wear after our little excitement, other than some leaves and twigs stuck in his fur that he must have picked up on his rush through the woods. However, when I got to his paws, I noticed something that looked like a few dead wood strips caught between his toe pads. Could he have? No, that's not possible.

Rush

When Dad tried to get me to go inside that box I was hesitant. Sure, I didn't really *want* to go in there, but that's not the only reason I was hesitant. I didn't like being cornered in there. I felt like it would be better if I was free to move. Dad hissed at me to get in. I didn't have time to explain it to him, like I could have anyway, so I ran just as fast as I could toward the trees. Yeah, baby! Rush was rushing!

I got far enough into the trees to keep out of sight but still able to see what was going on. After closing the box door on Dad, Southern Comfort went back over to the hut where I saw her grab something and shove it under the hut floor just as a truck came driving up the overgrown path. The truck stopped and out came Ranger Dick! I had to fight the urge to run down there and bite his hiking trip ruining ass!

LEE LOVELACE

I saw him talk to Southern Comfort, then look around the area. He peeked in the hut then walked over to the privy and opened that. Seeing nothing, he walked toward the box Dad was hiding in. Oh no, what if he opened it? Dad would be dog food, and not the good wet juicy kind, the crappy hard tasteless kind. I had to do something. But what? I surveyed the surrounding woods and glimpsed a huge dead tree leaning against a smaller dead tree. Dad calls these willow makers, or something like that. I looked back and saw that Ranger Dick was almost to the box. This was the only idea I had, so I moved as quickly and quietly as I could over to the dead tree.

I put my front paws up onto the lower trunk of the leaning willow maker and pushed as hard as I could. It shook and moved ever so slightly, but it didn't fall. Damn! From this position I couldn't see what was going on in the hut area, but I knew Ranger Dick would have that box open soon and we'd all be in for a shit storm. I switched tactics and shuffled up onto the leaning tree with all four paws. Trying to keep my balance, I bounced up and down. On the third bounce, the little dead tree snapped and freed the willow maker that came down with a tremendous crash! I went flying, rolling over multiple times through leaves and sticks.

I was dazed but I could hear Southern Comfort shout, "What was that?" Then I heard footsteps coming my way. I picked my dirty furry butt off the ground and slinked further back into the trees to hide. After that, I kind of zoned out for a bit. I guess I'd hit the ground a little harder than I thought. When I regained my senses, I listened. It sounded like Dad was talking to Southern Comfort and I couldn't hear Ranger Dick at all. Did it work? Only one way to find out. I made my way back to the hut area, keeping ears, nose, and eyes out for anything untoward. I reached the side of the hut without incident and slowly peeked around. There was Dad and Southern Comfort sitting on the edge of the hut floor. Dad hopped up, grabbed his walking stick and started looking to the trees I had disappeared into. I rounded the hut and when they both caught sight of me they beckoned me over. I ran over and couldn't help but fold into Southern Comfort's embrace first. Sorry, Dad, but she's so cuddly.

I eventually got over to Dad and let him hug me and do a pat down. He lifted my right front paw and pulled out a piece of the dead willow maker tree that had gotten stuck there. He looked at it and then looked at me. He had the weirdest expression on his face. *That's right! I saved your ass! You're welcome, MoMo!*

CHAPTER NINE

We'll Get By With A Little Help From Our (Hiker) Friends

Momo

"What now?" Southern Comfort asked me as we both sat on the edge of the shelter with our legs dangling off. Sawyer had retreated into the shady portion of the back of the shelter to lie down for a bit. He'd had a busy day so far. Hadn't we all?

"I don't know," I replied. "Our plan a few days ago was to get further north and see if we could get out. They are concentrating the search more in the southern district."

"How do you know that?"

"Because I took Ranger Dick's radio the other day when we had our, uh, encounter."

"Ha! Nice."

"The Swift Run Gap entrance and exit station is only like three miles from here and is always busy. I'm wondering if we can somehow get out among the crowd."

Southern Comfort sat there for a minute and appeared to be thinking about what I said. "How does this sound? I have to stop off at that station anyway to get a replacement thru-hike permit. I can check out the situation and then come back and let you know what y'alls chances are."

"Are you sure about that? I mean you are on a thru-hike and this has already had to put a hurtin' on your mileage."

100

"Are you kidding me? I went on a thru-hike for adventure, and this is shaping up to be a helluva one. It's not about the miles, it's about the smiles, and it would give me the biggest smile in the world to help you and Rush."

I chuckled to myself at her use of the well-worn turn of phrase but I was also very touched. "Wow, I love hikers. We are one-of-a-kind. You don't know how much this means to me, and I'm sure Rush would echo that sentiment if he were awake."

"You know the trail provides, and right now it's providing me. I'll be back in a couple of hours. Lie low. I don't think you'll get any more ranger visits and I'm sure any thru or section hikers showing up will be completely sympathetic to your situation, but day hikers might not know what is really going on and could turn you in."

That was solid advice, and I nodded my head in agreement. Southern Comfort geared up and headed down the blue-blazed trail. When she was out of sight, I sat about fixing us that lunch we had never gotten around to. Sawyer woke up to get some treats I offered him, then wondered off a bit to do some business. Seemed like a good time for that business, so I visited the privy myself to use it for something other than a place to hide. After that, I put everything back in both our packs to have them ready to strap on and beat feet if need be. Then we chilled, waiting for Southern Comfort to come back.

"Hey Rush," I said to Sawyer. "Keep an eye on things. I'm going to catch a little shuteye." He gave me a little huff and I stretched out in the shelter using my pack to prop my head on. A month ago, I would have never even entertained the thought of leaving Sawyer to his own devices while I napped. The dynamic had certainly changed and I realized we were more than just Master and Dog now. We were partners. It didn't take me long to drift off to sleep.

Sometime later I felt someone grab me! It was Ranger Dick! He *had* come back and caught us! He was stooping over me and shaking me awake. When he saw he had my attention he stood back up. What was that in his hand? It was my walking

101

stick and he was raising it over his head preparing to strike. He was going for a little payback. Wait a minute. Something was not right. As Ranger Dick swung my stick down toward me it morphed into a little branch. Instead of whacking me, Ranger Dick started pawing at me with the branch, dragging it back and forth across my right arm. What the fuck was this? As he continued to do that, Ranger Dick morphed also; into Sawyer! Then the haze fell away and I could see Sawyer pawing at me trying to wake me up. It had all been a dream.

"What is it Rush?"

Sawyer looked toward the blue-blaze trail and huffed. That's all I needed to know. Someone was coming. I looked at my watch and saw it had been a little over two hours since Southern Comfort had left. Hopefully, that was her coming back but I wasn't taking any chances. I strapped Sawyer's pack on and for once he stood perfectly still while I buckled it. I strapped my pack on, grabbed my stick and we both stepped down from the shelter so we would not be cornered if we needed to run.

Luckily, we wouldn't have to do that since it *was* Southern Comfort we saw strolling up the trail. I was happy to see her return but by the grim look on her face I knew the news was not good. She confirmed it when she said, "There is no way you are getting out at Swift Run Gap. They are checking every car leaving and there are a number of rangers spread out to prevent anyone from trying to skirt them through the woods."

"Well, hell," I said sighing. I unbuckled my pack and let it drop to the ground by the picnic table. What now? I sat down and tried to think. Sawyer came over and tried to get my attention but I was too deep in thought to notice.

"Let me get that Rush," Southern Comfort said and I looked over to see her pulling off Sawyer's pack. I couldn't help but chuckle at that.

"Well, if he didn't like you enough already, you just made a friend for life. He hates that pack."

She laughed at that and gave Sawyer some good scratches where the pack straps had been. Sawyer's eyes rolled back in his head as he enjoyed that massage. After a few minutes, she asked me, "Want to see something cool?"

I raised my eyebrows. She sat down, dragged her pack between her legs and started digging inside. She found what she was hunting for, drew it out, and showed it to me. In her hand was a radio that looked like the one currently residing in my pack. "What the fuck? Where did you get that?"

"When I was getting my new thru-hiker pass I noticed it sitting in the passenger seat of an empty ranger's truck that had the windows rolled down. When I left the station I reached in and grabbed it. Figured it might come in handy."

"Damn girl! You got some balls on you."

"Not the last time I checked," she laughed. "But thanks anyway."

An idea started forming in my head and I got quiet. After a few minutes I thought I had a viable plan and voiced it. "I think we should still try for Swift Run Gap but late at night. Things there are bound to be more relaxed then. So far we've avoided night hiking because I thought our headlamps would draw too much attention in the dark, but now that we have two radios we can work around that."

"How?" she asked.

"If you are still willing to risk your neck, you can hike up ahead of us, then Rush can hike in the middle, and I'll bring up the rear. You would meet anybody going southbound and I would encounter anyone catching up to us going northbound. Rush would be safe in between us. You can radio me if you come into contact with anyone and I can get Rush off the trail and turn off my headlamp. If someone comes from behind us I can do the same and radio you so you would know to hold up until they pass. We can make it this way to Swift Run Gap and hopefully Rush and I can slip by with you watching out for us and letting us know of any potential danger by radio."

I saw her think this through for a few minutes and then she smiled. "That might work MoMo. Let's give it a shot. We can hang here until we are ready to go. What time do you want to go?"

"Let's leave here around midnight; by the time we get there things should be pretty chill."

Southern Comfort gave me a thumbs up with one hand and kept scratching Sawyer with the other. Sawyer was laying there enjoying this immensely which is why he was probably as surprised as us when we heard a voice say, "Well if it isn't Southern Comfort."

Rush

I jumped up and whirled around to see a guy, a thru-hiker by the looks of him, walking up the trail into the hut area. He was young, about the same age as Southern Comfort, or maybe even younger. He had the typical thru-hiker long scraggly beard and was wearing a red bandanna tied over his head instead of the hats or caps you normally see.

I was pissed at myself for not hearing him coming. The scratches I was getting were so intoxicating I let my guard down. My sixth sense hadn't had a chance to let me know whether this was a good or bad guy so I wasn't taking any chance. I raised my hackles and uttered a low growl. The guy stopped in his tracks.

"Whoa Rush," Southern Comfort said. "I know him. He's a good guy."

I looked back and saw Dad had stood up with his walking stick in hand. At hearing Southern Comfort's words he relaxed and loosened his grip on the stick. My sense had kicked in now and I could also tell this guy was all right.

"Let me introduce you to Billy Idol," Southern Comfort said while sweeping her arm, palm up, toward the guy.

"Hey!" Billy Idol said. "Did I hear you correctly when you called the dog Rush?"

"Yeah. This is the infamous MoMo and Rush," she told him.

"Whoa, dude. Did you really attack a ranger? I mean I heard you had good reason but did that really happen?" Billy asked

Dad.

Dad went over the actual circumstances of the incident again for Billy's sake, downplaying my part in it as much as he could and I was grateful for that. After that they did the usual thru-hiker meeting routine and we learned that Billy Idol got his trail name because he was fond of doing a Rebel Yell. From what they said there was another hiker out here with that trail name so the other hikers bestowed Billy Idol on him because of the song. Billy and SC had been hiking together off and on and were just meeting up again after a few days apart. When she and Dad explained the plan we were going to put in motion, Billy wanted to help.

"I'm meeting a shuttle at Swift Run Gap to go into Harrisonburg to resupply and take a zero. I can tell the rangers there that I saw you two back at the entrance to the Two Mile Run trail to the south of here and maybe they'll take some of their resources there to go search the trail. It might give you the chance you need to slip through later tonight."

"That would be awesome!" Southern Comfort told Billy. "Thanks for the help."

"You know I'd do anything for you SC. If you vouch for this guy, that's all I need."

"You have my thanks as well Billy," Dad told him.

I expressed my gratitude also by rubbing up against Billy's left leg. He reacted by giving me a few ear scratches. They weren't as good as Dad's or SC's, but nice all the same. Billy refilled his water bottles and had a snack, then bid us goodbye and good luck before he headed out. Dad announced that we only had about an hour left of sunlight, so he and SC made dinner. They both cooked Mountain House meals to get some maximum calories before our nocturnal hike. I got my usual hard dog food mixed with a wet pouch, but even with Dad's hiker hunger, he let me have a bit of his Teriyaki chicken.

By the time dinner was eaten and everything put away, the sun had set and the light was running from the sky. We retreated to the shelter to bide our time. From my experience on the trail so far, I knew that it was unlikely that anyone else would show up after dark. It happened from time to time but that was unusual, and this occasion turned out to be no different. We were on our own.

I did a patrol, and took care of my nighttime business before settling down. I hopped down from the shelter and walked a circle around camp. Normally, Dad would have lost his shit if I had taken off from the shelter unleashed, but with our new partnership it was becoming routine and he didn't even think twice about it. Dad had pulled a pack of cards out and was showing SC how to play a game called 31. He and Mom played it all the time. I went and did my business in the woods and walked the blue-blaze trail back to the big trail. I didn't hear or smell anything out of the ordinary so I came back to camp, hopped up in the shelter near the entrance, and took up the night watch. *You guys can rest easy, Rush is on the job.*

CHAPTER TEN

Exit Strategy

Momo

While playing cards with SC, we chatted, and the subject turned to what it often does among long distance hikers. "Why are you thru-hiking?" I asked her.

"I get asked this question a lot. But it is usually more like *why is a woman hiking alone? Or* sometimes one will right out say *you are crazy to be hiking out here all by yourself, girl!"*

It was true. Even in today's world, there were far fewer female hikers than there were male ones, but the trend was changing. I'd read blogs and watched YouTube vlogs of some kick ass women hikers. Southern Comfort struck me as someone cut from the same cloth. "Ha! Well I'm not asking or saying that. You seem more than capable of taking care of yourself out here."

"Well, thank ya," she replied with that southern drawl. "What it boiled down to was that I spent a lot of time going to school to get a degree and then got a job sitting in a cubicle all day. After several years of that, I just felt like my life was being wasted living the *normal,"* she air quoted that word, "life. When I was in my teens, my family took a trip to the Great Smoky Mountains National Park. While we were there, I saw the AT for the first time at Newfound Gap. I only walked on it for a few feet, but I remembered thinking it would be really cool to hike

107

the whole thing one day. To make a long story short, I took a year to prepare, quit my job, and then set foot on the southern terminus of the Appalachian Trail at Springer Mountain in Georgia, without ever backpacking one single night in my life."

"Wow girl. You got guts. I don't think I could make such a drastic change in my life. Especially not at this age."

"Yeah, you could, if you really wanted to. You can't wait around to do the things you want to do. You never know how much time you have on this Earth. The only thing you have to do is stop coming up with reasons for not doing it, and start coming up with ways you can make it work."

That was a great way to think about the subject, and as we finished up our card playing and slipped into our sleeping bags, that thought was on my mind until I fell asleep.

I came awake at the touch of someone shaking me again. This time there was no dream. I could see that Southern Comfort was the one doing the shaking from the glow of the red light on her headlamp. Before we laid down to get a few hours' sleep she had set an alarm on her phone for 11:30 to give us time to get packed up before we headed out. I had considered using her phone to call my wife to let her know what was going on. Unlike most shelters that were usually located in a gap, High Top Hut was three quarters of the way up High Top Mountain, and SC had a couple bars of service. I decided not to make the call as much as I wanted to. While I'd guess they were looking to specifically track my phone's location if I was dumb enough to turn it on, they could be monitoring all voice communication between cell towers in the park's coverage zone. I couldn't take any chance that they would hear me talking to my wife and zero in on SC's phone.

"Rise and shine MoMo."

I grumbled a bit, but got up. I noticed Sawyer was already up and pacing around the shelter. We got our stuff packed and clipped our radios to a strap on our packs. Before we had gone to sleep last night, we had configured the radios so they were on the same frequency. We knew there was the possibility of us being overheard, but we were only going to use trail names and speak in code as much as we could. As a group we hiked back down to the AT.

"OK," SC said when we were standing at the intersection. "I'm going to head out. Remember to give me about ten minutes before y'all take off." I gave her a thumbs up and she started hiking north, the now white light of her headlamp bobbing up and down before it disappeared around a turn in the trail.

"Rush," I said to Sawyer. "I'm going to need you to hike ahead of me a little ways. I don't have a headlamp for you, not that you would wear it if I did, but luckily there is some moonlight for you to see by and I know your eyes are better than mine." He looked me in the face the whole time so I was hoping he got it.

After ten minutes, I told Sawyer to go on and pointed up the trail. Without hesitation he took off at a steady pace but not running. When he was just out of my sight I started walking. As I climbed my way up the mountain I kept alert for any noise behind me. I heard nothing and I guess SC hadn't either because the radio remained silent. I tried to keep Sawyer in my view, but with the limited range of my headlamp I could only spot a flash of his tail from time to time. This was my first time night hiking and it was definitely different. For one, it was hard to see, duh. You also had to slow your roll for fear of tripping on stuff you couldn't see. Every sound seemed to be amplified. Noises of critters in the woods that I wouldn't think twice about during the day, morphed into bears and mountain lions ready to pounce. Slow and steady was the order for the night, and in this way I continued toward the top of the mountain.

Rush

No headlamp for me? Damn, that would have been cool. No worries, you are right, my eyes are better than yours, not to mention my ears and nose. How the hell are you humans the dominant species? Anyway, I had no trouble understanding what Dad was saying and I headed up the mountain at a steady pace. It was easy to pick up Southern Comfort's scent as it was the freshest one, and this time of night, the only other human scents were noticeably stale.

I continued up the trail, now and then spotting a flash from Dad's headlamp behind me. I made it to the top of the mountain. It had been a steep climb and I was thirsty but my water was in the damn pack on my back so I would have to wait for Dad to get a drink. I waited for a few moments and didn't see him appear. He was probably huffing and puffing his way up the grade. I shouldn't be giving him such a hard time. He *was* carrying a much bigger pack than mine. That wouldn't stop me from having a little fun with him though. I left the trail and pushed my way into a bush so that in the dark I would be completely hidden. There I waited until I could hear Dad approaching and then shortly saw the bobbing of his headlamp. He passed right by me, taking several more steps before he realized he was at the summit of the mountain. There he stopped to catch his breath and take a few swigs from his water bottle. I slowly made my way up to him as he was facing away and stuck my head between his legs, goosing him.

"Yikes!" Dad uttered and jumped several feet. He whirled around framing me in the beam of his headlamp. "Sawyer! What the hell? That was not funny!"

Hey, use my trail name, Momo, and yeah, it was funny. I gave him my best smile and he couldn't help but chuckle a little.

"OK, it was a little funny but probably not the best idea when we're doing stealth operations here."

Just because we're fugitives doesn't mean we can't have a little fun. Now give me a drink! I shook the pack on my back which Dad knew by now meant I was thirsty. Before he did anything about it though he unclipped that box that had voices in it I now knew he called a radio, and brought it up to his mouth.

"SC, taking five," he said into the radio. I heard a single *click* from the radio which, I assumed, was SC's way of acknowledging

Dad without saying too much. Dad pulled some water out of my pack and gave me a drink in my bowl. He also took the time to take a few pulls on his water bottle. After a few more minutes he reached up to the radio again. "SC, moving on." Again there was the single *click* of acknowledgment from the radio.

Dad told me to head out and I did. I could hear him coming behind me several minutes later. I made my way down the other side of the mountain by the light of the moon. I was moving along for a bit when I heard a commotion behind me and saw Dad practically running down the trail as fast as he could by the light of his headlamp. He was barely maintaining control by leaning heavily on his stick. I stopped and he almost barreled straight into me.

"Rush! We have to get off the trail. Follow me!" he hissed at me in a low but urgent tone.

We scurried through the middle of some Rhododendron bushes and got still. Not long after I heard the sounds of someone coming from the direction we had been traveling on the big trail and I could see a white light bobbing along. A male SOBO thru-hiker approached our position then went by without a pause. We waited a little longer and Dad stood up and keyed his radio. "Clear," he said followed by a *click* of acknowledgment. Dad turned to me, "Not sure if he would have been a problem, but when SC spotted him she alerted me and we weren't taking any chances." *Good policy,* I thought. "OK. Let's get back to it. We're going to be coming up to a parking lot and crossing the big road again. SC is going to be there waiting for you if it is clear. OK?" I gave a huff and Dad took that as a yes.

I headed on the trail and down the mountain. I came out of the trees on to the big road and saw the parking lot across from it. I also saw SC beckoning me to join her. I looked both ways (yes a dog knows to do that, well, a good dog does) and ran to her.

"Good boy!" she said to me. "Let's get out of sight, Rush." We continued up the trail so we wouldn't be visible from the road and she stopped. "Let's wait for MoMo shall we?" She then gave me some of those killer ear scratches.

Momo

I waited a few minutes after Sawyer disappeared down the trail then started hiking after him. Southern Comfort had radioed me about coming across the SOBO hiker so we avoided him. She had let him pass and Sawyer and I did the same. More than likely he wouldn't have been a problem but we didn't have time to get into lengthy explanations.

As I came out of the tree line and approached the Skyline Drive, I didn't see either SC or Sawyer by the light of my headlamp. That didn't worry me. I knew neither one of them would want to stay exposed in the parking lot. I crossed over the quiet road, through the lot, and continued on the trail. I didn't have to go long before I saw SC bent down giving Sawyer some TLC. "Sorry to interrupt," I said as they caught sight of me.

"Har Har," she said, and I caught a smirk from Sawyer.

"Everyone ready for the next part?" I asked them.

"Yeah. We have about one mile to the gap. The trail comes out onto a bridge that crosses route 33. On the other side of the bridge is the ramp leading to route 33 and the entrance station."

I thought about it for a minute. "What's the tree cover like between where the trail comes out on the bridge and the embankment down to route 33?"

"From what I can remember, it's not too thick and goes pretty much all the way until you get to the road. There's probably about fifty yards of open concrete as it slopes down to the road."

"O.K. I'm thinking that's where we make our escape attempt. Hopefully most of the attention will be focused on the entrance station across the bridge and we'll be able to get under it and out."

"That's a good plan y'all. I'll go on over the bridge and be a lookout for you. I'll give you a click on the radio when I see that it's clear and alert you if I see any trouble coming your way. You ready to head out?"

I nodded to her, and she hiked. I felt like we were getting ready to split from an old friend. In reality, we hadn't even known her for more than a day. But that's how it was with hikers. You can spend a bit of time with someone you just met and feel like they have been your lifelong friend. "Wait SC," I said to her. She stopped and turned around. "We can't thank you enough for all the help you've given us. We'll never forget it."

Sawyer gave her a big smile and she returned the favor. "It's been my pleasure, MoMo and Rush. The only thanks I need is y'all getting out of here safe and sound. Now, let's do this before I start crying!" With that, she turned away and hiked on.

We waited and then spread out on the trail as before, covering the mile without incident. Sawyer had waited just before the trail opened up onto the bridge. I joined him and surveyed the area. It was just as SC had said. To our left the trees ran down to a concrete embankment making up the overpass to the bridge. I didn't see anyone around. I also didn't see SC but I knew she was keeping vigil on the bridge. Just then I heard the distinctive all clear *click* on the radio. I reached up and turned off my headlamp. We were going to have to use the moonlight for this last part. I patted Sawyer and told him to follow me as we did a small bushwhack through the trees down to the embankment.

We were going to be exposed for about fifty yards until we got under the bridge. Also, even though it was well past midnight, there was the occasional car rushing down route 33. We waited until we didn't see any cars and then ran full-out toward the underside of the bridge. Sawyer outpaced me and got there first. He instinctually took cover behind one of the concrete pillars that held the bridge up and I joined him. Panting and out of breath, I bent down and hugged Sawyer. "We did it, boy!" I huffed out. "We did it!" I reached up to my radio and gave the transmit button a brief squeeze to let SC know we were good. I got a *click* in return and I smiled. I knew that girl would make it to the summit of Kahtadin. I looked around to see what the best route down 33 would be for us when all of a sudden we were bathed in the brilliance of a thousand suns! I shielded my eyes and made out through the small space in between two fingers, the image of a ranger's green and white truck, and the headlights that were now spotlighting us.

Then I heard SC's voice from the radio. "RUN!"

Instinct took over again. I yelled, "Sawyer, run!" He took off across the bottom of the overpass and up again before I lost sight of him. The door of the truck opened. I unbuckled all my straps on my pack and let it fall to the ground. I tightened my grip on my stick and brought it up, prepared to engage Ranger Dick again. I doubted the outcome of *this* melee would go in my favor but I was giving Sawyer every advantage I could.

"You won't be braining *me* with that thing," a voice said. It was a female voice and as she cleared the high intensity of the headlight beams I could make her out. A red head that couldn't be more than in her late 20's dressed in a ranger's uniform. The most striking thing about her was the Sig Sauer service pistol she was pointing at me. "Drop the stick slugger," she said to me with almost a smirk on her face. I quickly judged the distance between us and knew there would be no chance of disarming her before she put a few holes in me. I dropped my stick and watched it roll to a stop halfway between us. One of the knot holes was turned toward me like a single eye with a helpless expression. The ranger approached me, turned me around, and applied some plastic hand restraints. I caught the smell of cigarette smoke in her uniform before she zipped the restraints up tight. It was not gentle.

Rush

"Sawyer, run!" Here we go again!

I took off under the bridge before whoever it was in the truck, probably Ranger Dick, could even get out. When I reached the other side I headed up the opposite embankment, toward the trees. Once I got into the cover of the trees I took a moment to look around. I was near the big road again. Across from it

I could see a little shack with several green and white trucks parked around it and a few people milling about. What should I do now? By the light of the moon I could see that the big trail continued along the side of the road and entered the woods again up the way. I could stay in the trees and move forward, eventually coming out on the trail. Should I go up the trail and find some place to wait for Dad like last time? Maybe I could find SC? Looking around I didn't see any sign of her. OK, head up the trail, find a place to hole up and someone would be along.

No! I wouldn't do that. What if Dad was in trouble? I ran for my life last time, this time I would not leave him behind. I made my way back over to the embankment and down again. I peeked around a big pole and observed the situation. There was a ranger walking Dad, his hands behind his back, over to the truck. It wasn't Ranger Dick, it was a woman. She opened the passenger door and put Dad inside, then crossed to the driver's side and got in. I couldn't let her take him away! I had no idea what to do but I stealthily made my way to the side of the truck. The windows were down and I could hear the ranger talking.

"So I guess you didn't get out after all," she said to Dad.

"Nope," was his only reply.

"Where did the dog go?"

"Who knows? Hopefully long gone from here by now."

I knew the sound of her voice! It was the female ranger that I had heard back at the ranger station when we were hiding in the old shack. From only the half profile I could see from my vantage point down beside the truck, I saw her pick up a radio of her own and put her finger on the little button that Dad pushed before he talked. She paused.

"Why would you attack a Ranger?"

Dad sighed deep and said, "I had no choice."

"What do you mean by that?"

"Ranger Dick was going to shoot my dog with a tranquilizer gun and take him away to put him down. All for killing a deer in the park."

The woman couldn't help but chuckle at the moniker we had

given the offending ranger. Then she caught herself like she wasn't being professional and ceased. "That would be Russell."

"Well, Russell is a dick."

"I'll neither confirm nor deny that statement, but it is against the law to kill a deer in a national park."

"I didn't kill the deer. My dog did and he did it on instinct. Yeah, I should have leashed him up better but what happened, happened. I wish it didn't but I don't think a death sentence is warranted for a descendant of a wolf that followed his instinct to hunt prey."

She paused a moment then said, "Did Russell actually say he was going to put your dog down?"

"Yeah, he did, then tried to tranq him. I had to defend him. What would you have done if you had been the ranger that came when I reported the kill? You know I could have just kept going on without saying anything."

"I wouldn't have handled it the same way he did, but Russell is a special case. He is one of the most senior rangers we have but he'll never go any higher because of his, uhm, shall we say, gung-ho tactics?"

"Are you telling me he is full of shit and he wouldn't have hurt Sawyer?"

"No, I'm not telling you that at all. He is fully capable of hurting your dog. But probably not in an official capacity. The problem is that's not the issue now. You attacked him, and even if you believe it was justified that's all anyone cares about now. The deer and the dog are secondary issues. You have to be taken into custody until this can be sorted out."

"Yeah, and in the meantime my dog is out there somewhere for Russell Ranger Dick to do whatever he wants to him."

I heard her pause and could see her trying to figure out what to say next.

"I have to call this in. I'm sorry, I have no choice." She raised the radio to her mouth again. This was when I decided I had to help Dad somehow. I didn't know if what I had planned was going to contribute anything toward that goal, but it was all I had.

I ran around to the back of the truck, increasing my speed, and took a leap into the back! I came down with a loud *THUMP* and *SCREECH* as the nails on my paws arrested my forward momentum.

"What the hell?" I heard the ranger say from inside the cab. She turned and looked at me through the window with a shocked expression on her face. She dropped the radio from her mouth. That was a good start.

"Sawyer, no!" I heard Dad say when he got turned around for a view. I knew he wouldn't like this, but I wasn't leaving him behind anymore. I uttered a small huff and tried to look as non-intimidating as I could. The ranger opened her door and came around to the back of the truck. "Just let him go!" Dad said.

"Relax, I'm not going to hurt him. What's his name?"

"Sawyer. He has a trail name too but I'll keep that to myself."

"Sawyer," the lady said to me. "I'm not going to hurt you. Can you come here?"

Yup! That was my plan all along, lady! I jumped over the side of the truck bed, darted by her, and up into the cab I went through her still open door. I made my way over to Dad and licked him all over the face. Dad tried his best to hug me but with his hands restrained behind his back all he could do was nuzzle my face. "You should've kept running," Dad said but I could tell he was glad to see me. I gave him a *wasn't going to happen* huff and some more licks. After that, I turned around to see the ranger staring at us from the open driver's door of the truck. I did my best to put on the big puppy dog eyes. Is there any chance in hell this is going to work?

The ranger lady stared at us for a bit while I could see the internal conflict playing out on her face. "I'm crazy. I can't believe I'm going to do this. I just can't be responsible that this dog might come to harm." I gave her one of my best Colebrook smiles.

"What are you going to do?" Dad asked her.

"I'm going to let you go but.."

LEE LOVELACE

"Thank you!" Dad interrupted her.

"Don't thank me yet. I am going to let you go, but you won't be able to get out of the park. There are rangers stationed up and down route 33 that would spot you. You'll have to go back up and find another way out. I'll give you a fifteen minute head start and then I have to call in a sighting. I'll say you went past me going east on 33. That should divert attention long enough for you to get clear of this gap. That's the best I can do, and it's all I'm willing to do. I could get fired for this. Take it or leave it."

"We'll take it!" Dad agreed.

She came over to the passenger's side and pulled Dad out of the truck. She cut his plastic restraints, but kept her hand near her service pistol. "Go now before I change my mind."

"Thank you! We'll never forget this." Dad said. She said nothing in reply but her look said we better get going. Dad picked up on that as well because he grabbed his pack from the back of the truck where the ranger had put it, buckled it up, grabbed his stick and told me to come on.

Momo

I led Sawyer up the embankment, but he got ahead of me and did the leading himself. It looked like he knew where he was going, so I followed. We had been so close to freedom only to have it snatched away. It could have been much worse. Sawyer really saved the day for us with that stunt he pulled. It was high risk but it paid off. I didn't want to speak right now but when he led us into a grove of trees across from the Skyline Drive from the entrance station and stopped, I reached down and gave him a big hug. He tolerated it for a few seconds then shrugged me off and looked at me like he was asking what now?

That was a good question. I took out the map, and by the red light of the headlamp I studied it. We were low on water and needed to refill our bottles. I saw that the South River Picnic Area was about three miles north on the trail. I was sure there

118

would be somewhere there to get water and if Ranger Redhead had told them we were spotted on route 33 then we had a good chance of no searcher encounters.

I wondered what happened to Southern Comfort? She had surely spotted the ranger truck below the bridge when she radioed her warning. The ranger had taken my radio and didn't offer to give it back. I wasn't going to stick around and try to get it back. So now I had no way of contacting SC. Hell, she had probably had enough of this adventure and was halfway to Harpers Ferry by now. Nothing for us to do but hike on to the picnic area, get some water, and then figure out our next move. I left the red light on my headlamp shining to reduce the chances of anyone spotting us. Now that we didn't have a lookout I couldn't chance the white light. It was very slow going and not without a few stumbles, even from Sawyer with his super-duper eyesight. With the slow pace we got to the picnic area in a couple of hours. It was still dark out, but it wouldn't be for long.

In the barely glowing light of the upcoming dawn, I spotted a water pump spigot and was relieved when I pulled up the handle and a steady flow of cool water emerged from the spout. I let Sawyer get right under it and he drank to his heart's content. I had a few handfuls myself and then filled our bottles.

I could hear Sawyer whip around and give a warning huff. I looked that way and saw a figure emerging from the barely visible light. I tensed up right away and tried to retrieve my stick from the ground where I had let it fall. Water splashed all over my shorts as I fumbled for it. Sawyer shot away and I thought he was going to try and save us from another ranger incursion, but I saw him duck his head and nuzzle the stranger.

"Hey Rush," I heard Southern Comfort say as she scratched his ears. She looked at me. "Hey pee pee pants, how the hell did you get out of this one?" I gave her all the details about how Sawyer had charmed Ranger Redhead and her only response was, "Holy shit."

"Indeed," I replied. "How did you know to come here?"

"I didn't exactly. I saw Rush take off and you get hog-tied. I figured you were finished but I was going to help Rush if I could. By the time I got to the trees on the other side of the bridge I couldn't find him. I figured he had moved up the trail. I looked at my Guthooks App and figured he might come here. I was waiting for quite a while and just about to give up when you two showed."

We took some time to eat a little snack. SC had a chocolate macadamia nut Cliff bar, Sawyer got a Puparoni treat, and I had a Snickers. SC was still hell bent on sticking with us and while I felt a little guilty for getting her involved, it also felt good to have an ally on our team. We were going on no sleep at all so we decided to try and find a stealth spot where we could get a few hours of shut eye. After about two more miles of hiking up the trail we came across an overgrown fire road. We hiked east on the fire road until we found a small clearing amongst a copse of trees just big enough to fit two tents. Inside our respective shelters we rested, relying on Sawyer's ears to alert us of any danger.

Rush

Relying on my ears, huh? No pressure or anything. Actually, not a problem. I let Dad fall asleep and I could hear Southern Comfort, well we won't call it snoring because it doesn't even compare to Dad's log sawing, settle into heavy breathing that indicated she was asleep herself. I stayed awake for a bit longer and then nodded off, but not before putting my ears in surveillance mode. Nothing alerted me and sometime later I awoke to the sound of SC moving around.

"MoMo, Rush, time to get up," she said through the closed door of our tent.

I got up and nuzzled Dad's face until he came awake himself. *Get up lazy ass! We got some planning to do.* Well, they had some planning to do. I had some staring, and smiling, and huffing to do at what they came up with.

Dad got his shit together and we emerged from the tent. Without words, they both set about breaking camp until everything was back in their packs and the evil one that was getting ready to adorn my back. Dad finally spoke up, "Any ideas?"

"Well," SC started. "Going on down the fire road is tempting but I know that's out of the question. They'll be watching the exits of the park on all of them."

Yup, good point there.

"I think we're just going to have to head north again. Hopefully Ranger Redhead's bogus sighting will have them thinking we got away and maybe things will cool off in a couple of days."

I spied my pack lying beside a tree and out of sight of the two planners. Should I? I think I should. I bit down on one strap and dragged the blasted torture device away, intending to hide it among the undergrowth.

"I don't know MoMo, Ranger Dick seems like a guy that holds a grudge. I don't think he'll give up that easy. Do you Rush? Rush? Where did he go?"

Crap! What a time for her to ask me a question. Dad looked around and caught me right in the act!

"Hey!" Dad yelled. "Not so fast there, pally-o!" He came over and tugged at my pack. I put up a token resistance but I knew it was to no avail, so I let it go. "Nice try!" They both laughed at me and I figured I wasn't going to get into any further trouble from the aborted heist attempt. They got back to the planning and I, defeated, laid down next to them.

"I agree," Dad said. "It's just that from my conversation with the ranger in the truck I get the feeling that not all of them are on board with Ranger Dick's obsession with this one. I think in a few days, especially if they think we got out, the search operations might be scaled back. Yeah, we might have to still deal with him, but wouldn't that be easier than dealing with a larger search force that probably won't be swayed by Rush's puppy dog eyes this time?"

Hey! Those puppy dog eyes saved your life buster! Don't doubt the power of those big round pools of hypnotic power. He was probably right though. Even those powerful weapons lost their effectiveness after being used too many times.

"OK, but I think night hiking is out without two radios and even if you hadn't let the Ranger Supergirl take yours, the battery on mine is almost done."

"So that leaves us with day hiking. We can still spread out some, just not as far apart as before. Head north, stay hidden, and take the pulse in a couple of days."

"How are you on food?"

"We can eke out a couple of more days I think. You?"

"I had just resupplied when y'all welcomed me at the privy. Between us, I'm sure we will be OK, for now."

"So we have a plan, agreed?"

"Agreed."

Agreed. Oops, I gave a huff of agreement instead.

CHAPTER ELEVEN

Stealth Meeting

Momo

For the next couple of days we all hiked north. In the same order as the night hike but not as spread out, we covered around fifty miles. We utilized the AT when we had to, went on side trails if they would lead us north, and sometimes even bushwhacked, especially when we knew the trail was going to cross Skyline Drive. We sneaked into shelters and read the logs. It looked like Billy Idol was back on trail and spreading all kinds of misinformation about bogus sightings of the infamous Momo and Rush. Others had taken up the deception as well. I was proud of my fellow hikers banding together for our sake. I was also proud of Sawyer. He hadn't been leashed in several days, and not once did I have to worry about him running off. He had truly transformed from a pet to a partner that was pulling his weight in this motley crew

We had a few scares running into people, but through our system of hiking we could avoid them. We once sighted a ranger's truck heading down a fire road we were about to cross but thanks to Sawyer's keen ears he had held us back and in hiding until it was gone. We listened to SC's radio when we could, but we didn't really hear anything that we hadn't before. It soon died and utilizing a plastic trowel for digging cat holes, we buried it in case someone came across it and fixed our location.

LEE LOVELACE

At one point, we took a series of side trails that led us up to the summit of Stony Man Mountain. We'd normally pass such areas as they attracted people, but it was in the middle of a weekday. There were no day hikers about and it seemed like the bubble of thru and section hikers had moved on. We sat for a spell and rested. At the summit of this mountain I could see the town of Luray spread out to the west below. I only knew it was Luray from the map, but it rekindled a memory.

Six years ago my wife and I had been visiting Colonial Williamsburg in Virginia. The people that worked there dressed up in Colonial costumes and stayed in character from that time period. They were holding an auction at the market. My wife had spied a cherry wood chess board among the items to be auctioned and wanted it. While I yelled out my bids to the old timey barker, competing with one other interested party, my wife had struck up a conversation with a woman who was sitting with a well behaved golden retriever by her side. A few minutes later I walked up to them, holding the chess board I had just won, and heard the woman saying that the beautiful dog was from Colebrook Farms in Harrisonburg. We both had always wanted a Golden Retriever and just a few months later we put a deposit down for a puppy. We had to wait several more months for him to be ready to go home.

When my wife and I had driven up to Harrisonburg to pick up little puppy Sawyer, we had come up a day before our allotted pick-up so we wouldn't have to drive back the same day with a rambunctious puppy in the car. Harrisonburg is just to the south of Luray and we visited the caves there. We had seen a brochure in the Residence Inn's lobby we were staying at for the night.

Then it hit me! I had an idea for getting us out of this park. "Hey!" I yelled, which was probably not the best idea in the world.

"What the hell MoMo?" SC said. "You want to do some yodeling too in case the rangers up in Front Royal didn't hear you?"

SAWYER'S RUN

"Sorry, sorry, but I have an idea."

This seemed to quell her dissatisfaction at my careless outburst. She raised an eyebrow as if to say, yeah? Sawyer also looked up from where he had been resting and was paying attention.

"Colebrook Farms," I simply said.

"And what in cotton pickin' name is that?"

"It's the place in Harrisonburg where we got Sawyer, I mean Rush, from. We are good friends with the owner. My wife started a Facebook group for people who got Golden Retrievers there, and we've kept in touch over the years. Her name is Tina and she loves animals, especially her golden boys, more than anything else. I'm sure she could help us somehow if we could only get in touch with her."

"You have her number? You can call her right now with my phone. I have an excellent signal up here."

Sawyer looked at me and I could swear he shook his head. "I don't think that would be a good idea. The rangers might be listening in on all communications coming from cell towers that cover the park. I doubt I could convey to Tina what we needed without making it obvious to someone who was listening."

We got quiet again as we tried to come up with a method of contacting Tina. Finally SC said, "I got it. We go old school."

"What do you mean?"

"When I went to the Loft Mountain wayside I saw an actual pay phone there," she said, consulting her Guthooks app. "Elk Wallow is the next wayside. It's about twenty-two miles from here. It's bound to have a pay phone. I'm willing to bet your two lives that they didn't even think about monitoring pay phones. I mean, who has *actually* used a pay phone in the last two decades? I can call her, and we can go from there." Sawyer gave a half huff/half bark of excitement. SC frowned and lightly thumped him on the nose. "Are you two bound and determined to get us caught when we just figured out how to pull y'alls asses from the frying pan?"

"So you are good with this plan I take it?"

125

"Hells yeah."

"Let's do it then."

It was already midday, so twenty-two miles was out of our range today. We camped near the Pass Mountain Hut which was half a mile off the AT. Hikers usually avoided unnecessary "sideways" miles when looking for a place to camp, so this one-mile trip would not count toward the trek northward. We would probably have the place to ourselves. We did. We put up our tents in stealth spots near the area so we could take advantage of the water source and privy.

The next day we were up early and heading north again. We covered the eight miles to the Elkwallow Wayside in a little over two hours. The excitement of enacting our plan had caused us to speed up our pace. About a mile before the wayside was a side trail called Jeremy's run. Sawyer and I went down this trail for about 0.2 mile and waited for SC to continue on to the wayside to make the call to Tina. As we waited, I started wondering who Jeremy was and why so many trails were called runs here. I looked at Sawyer and chuckled a bit. He fixed me with a quizzical look. "They should name a trail Sawyer's Run. You've certainly done enough running in this park to earn it!" I laughed and Sawyer gave me a smile and a huff of agreement.

SC was gone for about an hour. When she came strolling up the trail she had a big smile on her face which I took as a good sign. "Done deal!" she exclaimed.

When she didn't elaborate I said, "Give us the deets girl!"

"Well, she didn't answer the first two times I called but she did on the third. It took a few minutes to get her to understand who I was but when I mentioned Sawyer she immediately started taking me seriously. It took us a bit, and a few quarters, but we've arranged a meet. A couple miles up the AT is a side trail called the Tuscarora Overall Run Trail..."

"Ha! Another Run," I interrupted her.

"Huh?" Sawyer gave a huff and SC looked at us. "Inside joke between y'all?"

"Yeah, I'll explain it later. Go on."

"As I was saying... This side trail leads to the Traces Trail which circles the Mathews Arm campground. It's the middle of the week so I doubt there will be many campers. We're going to find a spot on that trail that is close to an empty campsite and wait for Tina. She's going to drive through the campground like she's looking for a spot and when we signal her she'll stop and we'll have our meeting and figure out where to go from there."

"Sounds like a plan! Let's do it!"

"Wait, I got you guys a present." She opened her pack and from within she produced a bag. I could smell it before she opened it. "I got us a couple of burgers at the wayside."

"You rock girl!" I told her as I greedily grabbed them, preparing to wolf mine down and break Sawyer's up in a few pieces for him."

"But wait," she said. "That's not all! Look what they had in a cooler." She withdrew two bottles of Devil's Backbone Vienna Lager.

"Oh. My. Gawd! I'm going to adopt you!" We removed the tops with my multi-tool and clinked bottles. "To getting the hell out of here. Things are finally looking up." As soon as the words were out of my mouth, I regretted them. Nothing like a good jinx to screw up a perfectly good beer. I put it out of my mind and enjoyed the rest of my fermented refreshment.

Rush

Oh boy, that burger was good! I wanted to adopt Southern Comfort too! When they clinked their beer bottles together and took a long pull, I saw the look of pure satisfaction cross Dad's face. He loves his beer.

We hiked on and I tried to recall some memories of Colebrook Farm where Dad said they got me from. I remember being with all my sisters and brothers in a pen at one point. I also faintly remember a woman who used to take us out and put us in those pens and feed us. That must have been Tina. I remember when

Mom and Dad came to pick me up. It seemed faint, but I had a vision of two people bending over the pen and I was in there with several brothers. I had two sisters and people took them already. I could see them picking up my brothers and then me. I liked them immediately and let them know by giving them licks. *I choose you guys* I tried to say but, of course, it just came out as a little high-pitched yip. They both said *this is the one*. I have been with them ever since. I'm so glad they agreed with my choice.

I really hadn't been paying attention (bad dog) while I was ruminating and I ran right up on SC standing at the intersection of a trail. Soon Dad appeared and we took the turnoff and spread back out a bit. In this manner we also made it to the circular trail that Dad and SC had been talking about that went around the campground. We came to a particular spot where we could spy a campsite through the trees that wasn't too far from the trail. We bunched up and moved through the trees toward this spot. Keeping vigilant (yes, I do know what it means), we approached and saw the campsite was empty as were the ones to either side of it.

"Guess we can wait here," SC said.

"Yeah," Dad replied. "And get ready to run if we see any green and white trucks."

I thought that was an excellent plan. I'm not sure how long we waited but it didn't seem all that long when we heard an approaching vehicle. SC tapped me on the collar and motioned for me to follow her back in the trees. I looked over at Dad and he gave me a nod, so I went. When we got back, I looked around the tree we were hiding behind and saw Dad crouched behind the picnic table at the camping site. A blue van came into sight. I could tell the driver was looking at all the sites. Dad flashed us a quick thumbs up and then stood up and strolled toward the road that wound its way through the campground. He waved a hand over his head and motioned for the van to come there. The van pulled in and a lady got out. She seemed familiar from my vision earlier so it must have been Tina. Without even a greeting she pulled back the sliding door on the van while saying something

SAWYER'S RUN

to Dad. Dad turned toward us and waved us over, and he jumped in the van. SC and I took off, and as I outpaced her, I nimbly leapt into the open door of the van and up on the back seat next to Dad. SC followed, sliding in the seat in front of us, and Tina closed the door and got back in the driver's seat.

Momo

"Stay in the back," Tina said to me and the others. "The windows are tinted back there."

"Southern Comfort," I said. She looked back at me. "There is no need for you to go with us any further. If we get caught you'll go down too and..."

"No fucking way!" she interrupted me. "Sorry for my potty mouth, Tina, but I left y'all before and I'm not doing it again. I'm with you for the long haul. If my ass gets caught, it gets caught."

I sighed but it didn't sound convincing. "All right, then. Have it your way you hard-headed country bumpkin!" She gave me a smile I couldn't be frustrated with. There was a big part of me that was glad she was being difficult. "By the way, Tina, meet Southern Comfort. SC, Tina."

Tina, who was a no-nonsense tough mountain woman, said, "Nice to meet you. We can do proper introductions when I get you the hell out of here. For now, get down."

SC dropped to the floorboard in front of us. Sawyer and I both tried to go down at the same time. All we did was bump heads. As I rubbed my skull, Sawyer gave me an exasperated look that acknowledged we both wouldn't fit there. Before I could say anything, Sawyer leapt over the seat into the small cargo area in the back where we had stowed our packs. He nestled down amongst them. "That'll work," I told him.

"What are you two doing back there?" Tina yelled from the front. "I'm getting ready to leave the campground."

"We're all good!" I responded as I ducked down.

All I could see was the top of trees and patches of sky from my vantage point as the van pulled out of the campground and on to Skyline Drive. It felt like we took a right coming out. Why would she take us back south?

As if sensing that very thought in my head Tina spoke up, "I came into the park at the Swift Run Gap entrance on 33 coming out of Harrisonburg. I didn't see them checking anyone that was leaving. When I passed Thornton Gap entrance as I drove north, I didn't see them checking anyone leaving there either. They must think you aren't in the park anymore. That's the closest exit, so we'll go there. Should be able to get you out no problem." Nobody said anything in return. I know all three of us, human and canine alike, were thinking the same thing. *Been there, done that, always a problem.*

As we traveled down Skyline Drive, I relaxed. It's not the reaction I thought I would be having. Instead of feeling wound up and nervous at the impending escape attempt, for who knows how many times (it seemed like the thousandth), I was having visions of Sawyer and me back home sitting by the fire with my wife in winter time. SC was there too, she had visited after completing her thru-hike. It seemed real and I barely registered it when Tina said, "Shit!" *She didn't just say shit did she?* Come on, tell me things weren't going south (figuratively) again. "Shit, shit!" she said again and I knew south in to the privy is where they were going.

"What?" SC asked her from the floorboard of the row ahead of us.

"Just stay down. There is a van with *Open Arms Hostel* written on the side and it's stopped at the exit station. I can't tell if they're searching it or just talking to them."

I pulled myself out of my Hallmark Moment vision and said, "Just keep going on the Skyline for now."

"That's what I am going to do. There is a big parking lot just down the road. I'm going to pull in there so we can figure out what to do."

A minute later I felt the van slow and veer to the right before slowing to a stop. "You can sit up," Tina said. "As long as you stay in the back we should be fine."

Yeah, *fine* didn't seem to be doing the trick. She had said it would be fine getting out of the park. I know it wasn't her fault, but I couldn't help feel frustrated once again. "What happened? I thought they weren't stopping vehicles that were leaving when you drove by earlier?"

"They weren't and I'm not even sure they stopped this van. I didn't see anyone searching it. It could be that they stopped on their own for some reason."

"Damn," SC said. "I'm never going to get rid of you boys."

I looked over at her to see she was smiling. This just frustrated me more. "What's with the shit-eating grin?" I asked her.

She winced a bit and I immediately felt guilty for that question. "Come on MoMo. At least you didn't get caught this time did you?"

She had a point. "OK, sorry. You're right. Guess we better come up with plan Z. We are going to have to start using numbers for these soon." I smiled at her.

"There ya go, hon. That's more like it."

Before we could even get started on plan Z, Sawyer started pawing at my back. I turned around to see what he wanted. He looked at me for a second and then scratched at the back door to the van. I knew this routine. He had to pee. Great timing there bud! I informed the others of Sawyer's requirement and took my first good look out of the windows at the parking area. It was more than just a parking lot. There were bathrooms here and water fountains. There was also a side trail here that ran down to the AT according to a sign next to where it started on the other side of the parking lot. There were a few people milling about, even a few hikers, but I didn't see any green and white trucks, rangers, or other official looking personnel. We should have found a more private place for this, but I was in a hurry to come up with a new plan and thought we could risk a quick pit stop for Sawyer's full bladder. "Come on," I said to Sawyer. "Let's get this over with, and there *is* a need to Rush!"

Rush

Puhleeze MoMo I thought at Dad. *Hardly a time for lame jokes.* I couldn't help I had to pee. With all the excitement today I had forgotten to take care of that little task. Now, with the letdown over the latest failed escape attempt, my bladder reminded me it needed draining.

Dad opened the sliding side door of the van and motioned me out. I jumped out and looked around. Normally, with our new-found trust, I would have sauntered off on my own, but in this parking lot it was a lot less woodsy and a lot more buildingy. I hesitated for a second, wondering where to go when Dad hopped out behind me.

"Come on," he said. "Around behind the bathrooms." He reached a hand out and grabbed the loop on my pack. I'm sure it was for appearance's sake. Hell, it had been so long since there had been a leash hooked to the harness it rode on I doubt Dad even knew where in his pack it was. Why was I still wearing *my* damn pack when we were in the van anyway? Might have to have a bark at Dad for that but it would have to wait. I was really feeling the urge now and led the way around the back of the bathroom building. There wasn't anyone there so Dad just turned me loose to do my business, which I gladly conducted.

When I was done, I trotted back over to where Dad was leaning against the back of the building waiting on me. "'Bout time," he said. *Whatever, let's get back and start working on this plan Z of yours.* As we were walking back around the side of the building with a door and a picture of a little stick figure man next to it I could hear a familiar voice coming from the open row of windows near the roof.

"You can't wash your dirty socks in here!" the voice said. "I have the authority to kick you out of this park for doing that."

I looked up at Dad. He looked down at me. Yeah, he knew too.

CHAPTER TWELVE

Sawyer's Run

Momo

I f I had any doubt, Sawyer's look erased it. Before either of us could react, the door opened and out came a recently chastised male thru-hiker (I knew the feeling), followed right behind by Ranger Dick. He stopped in mid-sentence about wanting to see the hiker's permit when he locked eyes with me. He took a quick glance down at Sawyer then turned his whole face into an awful grin. "You!" he screamed and went for his service pistol. I instinctively went to bring my hiking stick up for another go round and came up with empty air. I had left it in Tina's van along with my pack! Fight gave over to flight and I yelled that all too familiar phrase, "Run, Sawyer!"

If things had gone even slightly differently, I am sure this story would have ended there. Ranger Dick had malice on his mind when he cleared his pistol as Sawyer took off and I ran behind. I tried to stay in the line of fire between him and Sawyer as I ran, wondering what it would feel like when the bullets penetrated my body. Instead, I heard a scuffle and cursing. I risked a quick glance behind me and saw both the hiker and Ranger Dick in a heap on the ground. Ranger Dick was screaming at the hiker to get off him as he tried to extract himself from the entanglement. I didn't get to see how it happened, and it may have been an accidental collision, but I'd like to think the hiker recognized us as the much written about

133

MoMo and Rush in the trail logs, and wanted to help. Hell, he may have been pissed at Ranger Dick for the verbal abuse he had suffered and purposely was a little slow getting out of the way. No matter what the reason, it gave us the chance we needed.

Sawyer raced back out to the parking lot. The back door of the van was open where SC rummaged around in her pack. I knew we didn't have much time before the pursuit would commence again. As Sawyer neared the van I yelled, "To the big trail Rush! To the big trail!" He only took a second to get his bearings and altered course to cross the parking lot toward the side trailhead.

By this time the girls had noticed our all-out sprint, and Southern Comfort's face took on a quizzical expression after I had directed Sawyer to the trail. I, however, continued directly to the van and as I got in audible range, SC asked me what was going on, but I ignored her and continued right up to the back of the vehicle. There, without even breaking stride, I looped an arm through one strap on my backpack and continued running toward the trailhead, dragging it behind me. Before I got out of earshot I yelled, "We are on our own this time, SC!"

I knew all was probably lost and the one thought I had as Sawyer closed the distance to the van, had been limiting the girl's liability. Sawyer and I were toast. Tina and SC may only get lightly browned and talk their way out of any repercussions, but only if we separated now. When I had detoured Sawyer toward the trail I had intended to follow right along, but another thought hit me. If we managed to make it out of this one, we were going to need the contents of my pack to survive. I briefly entertained the idea of grabbing my stick, but when I had snatched my pack I could see the stick had rolled up under the back seat and I didn't have time to retrieve it. All this time it had been as faithful a companion as Sawyer had, but here we parted ways.

By the time I got to the side trail, Sawyer had already ran ahead. I glanced back and saw Ranger Dick, pistol drawn, halfway across the parking lot. I didn't waste any more time on observation and ran down the trail. I don't know how I did it, because I have difficult enough time doing it while standing still, but I got my pack strapped on and all buckled up while continuing to run. The side trail is just a short distance from the AT and as I neared the intersection I could see Sawyer stopped to look at me. A right turn would take us north back toward the Thornton Gap station. There would be more rangers there and the last thing I wanted was for Ranger Dick to get reinforcements. So south it would be. "Go that way!" I yelled at Sawyer while pointing left. He immediately took off in the indicated direction.

A moment later I reached the intersection and slowed a bit to make the left turn when I heard the pursuit behind me. I didn't look, but I knew Ranger Dick was coming. I made the turn to the south and picked up the pace. The trail ascended. We had come this way yesterday, only going north, and I knew it was a thousand foot climb. Sawyer had no trouble with it and was soon out of sight. Before beginning this section hike I would have been caught on this upgrade. But I'd been climbing up and down mountains for months now and I had a good set of trail legs on me. It still took some effort, and I was panting, but I continued a steady pace up.

At first I could hear Ranger Dick behind me, but as I continued up, the noise of the pursuit fell off. I remembered when I had been leading him to the dead deer and he was not in shape like the hikers he loved to harass. I gained some distance on him. Before long, I was at the top of the mountain. Here was a sign that said MARY'S ROCK 0.1 MILE and an arrow pointed west. We saw this yesterday, but passed it since, according to the map, it led to some cliffs and stopped there. I had no idea where Sawyer was. I had a decision to make—continue down the trail where we would eventually run into cohorts of Ranger Dick, or turn down this side trail and hope he passed it by, giving me some time to figure out what to do next. I chose the latter of the two options.

The trail here was very rocky and wouldn't show footprints indicating where I had gone. I slowed my pace a bit so as not to cause any noise that Ranger Dick could follow. A short walk later I emerged from the trees onto a beautiful cliff-side with an amazing view of the valley below. If I hadn't been running from a deranged ranger, I would have taken it all in. As it was, I only had time to give it a momentary appreciation before I ducked behind a large rock that made up part of the cliffs. I slipped my backpack off and wedged it under another rock outcropping to keep it from tumbling down the cliffs. I didn't want to be wearing it if there was going to be another encounter with Ranger Dick. Turns out there *would* be an encounter, just not with the aforementioned dick head.

As I was peeking over the top of the rock to see if Ranger Dick had come down the trail, I heard a rustling and grunting. *Great!* However, it was not him that broke from the cover of the trees. It was a huge black bear and her cub strolling along. The bear was sniffing among the rocks, maybe looking for dropped hiker treats. Her cub was wandering around near the opposite tree-line. I knew not to run from a black bear, hell there was nowhere to run. You were supposed to stand your ground and make a lot of noise. Usually the bear would just go the opposite way. However, all that advice had been predicated on the fact that you weren't on the run from a homicidal ranger. I couldn't make noise! As of yet, the mama bear had not noticed me crouching behind the rock but she was going to make her way over here soon and if I surprised her it might go badly for me. I stood so she would see me before she got to my hiding place. Keeping a steady gaze on her I waved my hands.

"Got you motherfucker!" I heard. I turned to the source of that invective and saw Ranger Dick standing there, pistol leveled at my center mass. In his zeal to get me, he had not even noticed the ursine presence.

"Watch out, there..." I tried to warn him, but he cut me off.

"Shut the fuck up!" He quickly crossed the distance between us and put himself directly between the mother bear and her cub. Without another word, he shifted the pistol around in his hand and whipped me square in the face with the butt of it. Pain erupted in my head and stars filled my vision as I tasted blood in my mouth. My knees became wobbly and I couldn't maintain my standing position any longer. I fell back among the rocks of the cliff experiencing new sensations of pain as parts of my body bounced off the hard surfaces. Sliding over the edge of the cliff, I flailed my arms around as the ground dropped from beneath me. Just before I fully went over, I caught a strap on my pack where it was wedged in among the rocks. This arrested my impending plunge and I held on for dear life!

"How did that feel?" Ranger Dick asked as he loomed over me hanging there. "Not a stick, but I bet it still packed a punch, huh? Where is that mutt of yours? He's next."

I was too scared to reply. I looked up as he stood over me. I didn't know what he intended to do. Pull me back up to safety and then to custody, or to stomp on my hands clutching the strap to my pack, sending me over the side to my death. If he was trying to decide between those two options he never got the chance. With a ferocious growl, mama bear charged Ranger Dick! Only now he noticed the bear's presence and whirled around to meet her. He fumbled to get the pistol turned around, but wasn't fast enough. The bear took a swipe and solidly connected with his arm. There was a different roar as the pistol discharged before flying out of Ranger Dick's hand. The bullet struck one of the big rocks and ricocheted into the ground. Ranger Dick spun from the force of the impact and mama jumped on his back, pinning him down.

I took this opportunity to pull myself up from the cliff side. It was difficult pulling my body weight up by one strap of my pack, but it was that, or a one-way ticket to the depths below. As I got to the edge, I heard a horrifying rip as the strap gave way and ripped from my pack exposing the contents inside. As I started to slip back over the edge I flailed my free hand about and got hold of a rock outcropping. Using this as an anchor, I pulled myself up, and dragged my ripped pack along with me. Now back on terra firma, albeit on hands and knees, I saw that Ranger Dick was curled into a ball. The bear was jumping up and down on him keeping him pinned on the ground. What was I going to do, let the bear rip him apart? Like I had a say in the matter when it came to *letting* a bear do anything. A part of me wanted the bear to rip him apart for all the pain and suffering he had caused us, but I wasn't that cold-blooded. I just didn't know what to do. Then I saw a golden blur burst from the tree-line!

Rush

As I ran by the turnoff to the blue-blaze trail I didn't even think about turning down it. I just continued on the big trail. The trail went down and I figured I could get to the bottom of the mountain, find a place to hide, and wait for Dad. We were in desperate need for that plan Z now. Several twists and turns later, I heard a loud bang. That was a gunshot! I've heard them before when Dad was visiting his parents on their farmland and was target shooting. This was not good. Did Ranger Dick shoot Dad? I needed to know what the hell was going on, so I turned around and ran back up the trail.

As I neared the turnoff, I could hear some noises and I smelled a foreign but familiar scent. It was a bear! What is going on here? I turned down the side trail and slowed my pace so I could approach the source of the sounds and scent. As I got to the end of the tree-line I came out on a surprising sight. A bear was attacking Ranger Dick and had him on the ground. I couldn't see Dad anywhere. For just a moment I enjoyed seeing this guy get the shit beat out of him, but then instinct kicked in again, just like it had when I went after the deer. A red-hot feeling of protective fury burned in me and even though the guy was a dick, I had no choice but to help.

I ran forward barking at the top of my lungs and lunged at the bear! Before it could turn around to face me, I bit down hard on its left hindquarters. The bear shrieked and with a mighty shrug of its rear, threw me off. I landed on the ground, rolled once, and was immediately back up on my feet. The bear turned to face me and forgot all about Ranger Dick. We both raced toward a point of impact and as the bear rose up to take a swipe at me, I ducked under and bit into its furry belly. The bear screamed again and dropped its whole weight down on me! It drove the air from my lungs and I let go. Sensing the release of my teeth, she got up and moved away to assess the damage to her belly. I drew in a huge breath of air that helped to clear my oxygen deprived brain.

In a far off place I could hear someone yelling, "Sawyer, no!" But it was only a periphery buzzing in my consciousness. The bear finished surveying its wounds and it was not happy at all at what it found. She bellowed an awful roar and came for me! I rushed forward to meet the challenge and tried to pull my ducking trick again, but she wasn't fooled and caught me a wallop with one of her huge paws. It felt like I had been hit with a brick and I went flying, landing on the ground hard where I laid dazed. Not wasting this chance, the bear pounced on my back, opened its big maw, and bit down. Agonizing pain shot through my body! It was like nothing I had ever felt before, not even when I had once toppled over the wood pile in the backyard and been pelted with logs. The pain was unbearable and things got fuzzy. The bear let go but only for a moment before it reached down and positioned its powerful jaws around my neck.

Momo

From my hands and knees, I watched in horror as Sawyer and the mama bear fought. I knew Ranger Dick was still lying on the ground. I saw Sawyer get in a few good bites but he was no match for a bear. I needed to do something, but what? Every second I hesitated, the bear was getting the better of Sawyer. I thought about my knife that was affixed in a scabbard to one strap on my pack. Did I think I stood a chance against a bear with a knife? No, I didn't, but if I could give Sawyer a chance to get away from the attack I was going to take it, no matter what it cost me.

I reached over and pulled my torn pack over to me, spilling

its contents all over the ground. Where was the damn knife? I couldn't see it. I tipped the pack over to see if it had been pinned underneath, and one more item fell out with a *thunk* on the ground. When I saw it I forgot all about the knife. There, lying on the ground, was the tranquilizer gun that I had taken off Ranger Dick way back when all this mess had begun. I had stuffed it in my pack where it had stayed; forgotten. I snatched it and examined it. I'd never used a tranq gun before, but the operation looked straightforward. There was a CO_2 cartridge attached to the gun and a small spring-loaded knob on the back. There was a dart loaded from when Ranger Dick had been ready to use it on Sawyer.

I pulled back on the knob locking it in place with a click. Then I got to my feet and turned toward my target. The bear had Sawyer on the ground and was biting his back! I had to do this now because he was seriously injured as I saw blood flowing from where the bear had bitten him. I brought the tranq gun up and sighted in on the bear. I only had one chance and my hand was shaking. The bear rose up for a second and then back down with her massive jaws closing over the back of Sawyer's neck. No! No more time for nervous second guessing. I made my final sighting, took a deep breath, and pulled the trigger.

I heard a hiss as the cartridge released CO_2 gas, propelling the dart out of the barrel of the gun. The dart flew true and embedded itself deep in the left hindquarter of the bear. She aborted her death chomp on Sawyer, let out a bellow, and faced me. Shit! How long did it take this tranquilizer to take effect? Oh well, at least I had kept her from chomping down on Sawyer's neck. The bear started coming toward me with harmful intent in her eyes. Halfway to where I was standing, those eyes fogged over. The bear stopped and shook her head a few times. She whined (which was still a scary sound) and turned around. Weaving like she was drunk, the bear sauntered off back into the tree-line. A second later, her cub came down from a tree it had climbed when the melee started, and ran after her, mewling cries drifting out of earshot as it followed its mother's track.

I ran to Sawyer's side and knelt down. "Sawyer! Are you OK?" I yelled. He didn't respond. I examined him and could see blood soaking his fur. He had a terrible scratch across the side of his face where the bear had swiped him. I gently shook him and called his name over and over but he laid still. Then I heard some movement at my back and turned around to see Ranger Dick stirring. This motherfucker had caused all of this! He was going to pay. I looked around and it didn't take me long to locate his service pistol the bear had knocked from his hand. I rose, took a few steps, and scooped it off the ground. I walked over to where Ranger Dick had gotten himself into a sitting position. He didn't even look that hurt. Just a few scratches. I had given him worse than that before and I planned to give him a lot worse now. I raised the pistol and pointed at him.

"You miserable piece of shit!" I yelled at him. "Do you know what you've done?" He raised his hands as if he could ward off the bullet I had planned for him but he said nothing. "You killed my dog! He saved your worthless life and now he is dead!"

He finally found his voice and there was no *authority* in it when he said, "I.. I'm sorry."

"Well, enjoy the few seconds of that saved life you have left." I stooped over and leveled the pistol a few inches from his forehead. He closed his eyes tight and I hesitated. Could I do this? End a human being's life? The answer shocked me but I knew it was true. I *could* and I was going to. As I tightened my finger on the trigger, I felt something tug at my arm that was holding the pistol, pulling it down. I looked over and there was Sawyer, bloodied and beaten, with his paw holding my arm down. I looked him straight in the eye and he gave me a barely perceptible shake of the head.

I lost all thoughts of revenge and dropped the pistol to the ground as I bent down and hugged Sawyer to me. He let out an involuntary yelp as I accidentally aggravated one of his wounds. "Sorry, buddy! Are you all right?" He looked at me and struggled mightily to give me one of those Colebrook smiles. I cradled him in my arms telling him he would be OK. We would get him help. I was so happy he had come back to me. "I love you so much, Sawyer." He gave me a feeble huff and then slumped to the ground to move no more. My walking stick hadn't saved him after all.

CHAPTER THIRTEEN

No Choice

Momo

I held Sawyer's body in my arms as tears of grief streaked down my face. I heard scuffling sounds behind me, and I turned to see Ranger Dick with the pistol in his hand. All thoughts of a fight had fled. Nothing mattered anymore. "Do what you want," I told him. "I don't care anymore."

He looked at me for a moment and then said, "I have no choice."

CHAPTER FOURTEEN

*I Fought The Law And
The Law Won*

Eight Months Later

Momo

The guard pressed a button on the control panel, opening the final gate and wished me well as I stepped outside. Sitting in the visitor's parking lot of the minimum security federal correction institute in Petersburg, Virginia was my jeep I hadn't seen in a long time. Standing next to it with a big smile on her face was my wife, whom I hadn't seen since last week during visiting hours. I ran to her, dropping my plastic bag of belongings they had given me upon release. I grabbed her tight and gave her a long kiss.

"Hey," I said.

"Hey yourself," she replied. "You want to drive?"

"Hell yeah!" I grabbed the plastic bag and tossed it into the backseat as I settled into the driver's seat. My wife got in on the passenger side.

"You ready?" she asked.

"More than you know."

I pulled out and headed for our destination. We held hands as I drove and I reflected on the last eight months. They had taken me into custody after our misadventure in Shenandoah National Park. They charged me with assault of a federal official. I plead guilty, and the judge took the extenuating circumstances into consideration when he sentenced me to three years incarceration in a federal facility since the crime had happened in a national park. My family and friends muttered shocked exclamations when the sentence had been read. I was surprised too, but I had no time to worry about it before the judge explained that all but six months of my sentence would be commuted if I served with good behavior. Turns out the judge owned three golden retrievers. Something my lawyer had found out before the hearing.

Our destination was slightly over a two hour drive and we spent that time getting caught up. We reached our destination, which was a big house in the shadows of the Shenandoah Mountains. As we pulled into the driveway I could see the sign COLEBROOK FARMS swinging from a post at the head of the drive, and the kennels erected in the backyard with the picturesque mountain scene as a backdrop. We came to a stop and I stepped outside. The door to the house opened and out came Tina, Matt, Chuck, and Southern Comfort. Tears flowed. I was happy to see them, but they were not the recipient of my waterworks. That recipient came trotting behind them. I ran forward as a golden furry face raced toward me. We met in the middle of the front yard and I embraced him as he put his paws around me.

"I missed you so much Sawyer!" I cried. Sawyer released me and jumped up and down and all around in pure ecstasy! I jumped around too and danced the happy dance.

"That's not Sawyer," my wife reminded me. "Only Rush from now on."

Oh yeah, I had forgotten. Sawyer was dead. Rush was alive and well!

As I had lain devastated at the base of Mary's Rock holding Sawyer's lifeless body eight months ago, Ranger Dick told me he didn't have a choice. The choice he didn't have was to do right by the dog that had saved his life. As a ranger, he had medical and veterinary training to treat injured animals encountered in the park. He convinced me to release Sawyer so he could examine him. After a few minutes, he told me something I didn't believe. Sawyer wasn't dead. He was alive, but only barely. Together we made a litter from the remnants of my backpack and carried Sawyer down to the parking lot. Tina and SC met us halfway down the trail. SC had guessed correctly that we wouldn't turn north towards the other rangers at Thornton Gap. They helped us carry Sawyer back to the parking lot. We put Sawyer in the back of Tina's van as Russell gave her and SC an escort out of the park where they raced him to Tina's vet. I found out later that the major wound on his back was not immediately fatal for a reason. Unbelievably, his hated backpack had taken most of the damage. That pack he reviled and had even tried to get rid of, had, in the end, saved his life. He was still seriously injured, and it was touch and go for a while, but the vet nursed him back to health.

I had remained with Russell in his truck. "This is what I can do," he told me. "Nobody knows what happened up there. I am going to tell them the bear killed your dog and pushed his remains off the cliff. Even if they search for him, by the time they get to that remote area, scavengers can explain his lack of presence. I doubt they will try though. They won't want to waste resources."

At this I gave him a hard stare, not liking his choice of words. "That brings you to me, right?"

He sighed, "Right. This has gone too far to forget about. The federal authorities would still hunt you down whether or not you got out of the park. You are going to have to take the hit but I'll give a statement about how your dog saved my life and hopefully it will help. I'm not promising it will, but it's the only thing I can do."

Was I supposed to say thank you? That wasn't happening. "OK," is all I got out.

Most of the rest you know already. When Sawyer was well enough to go home, Tina kept him at her place so she could blend him in among all her other goldens. As far as anyone who wanted to confiscate a "dangerous animal" was concerned, he no longer existed. This dog I was now dancing with would only be known by *Rush* from now on and that was just fine with me. Except for the hearing, when he made a statement as to how Rush saved his life, I never saw Russell again. I didn't speak to him then and I don't plan on ever doing it in the future. He did the right thing in the end, but if it wasn't for him there would have been no end to worry about. I hoped he learned a valuable lesson and applied it to his ranger duties in the future.

We spent a few hours visiting with everybody. Neither Southern Comfort nor Tina had born repercussions for helping me. With the assistance of Russell, Tina had convinced the other rangers that she was giving hikers a ride to a hostel, and SC didn't even know us. SC had eventually continued on her thru-hike and summited Kahtadin. I got a postcard from her in prison with a picture of her at the iconic sign at the northern terminus of the Appalachian Trail. In the body of the postcard she had written...

This was one of my finest accomplishments but it doesn't hold a candle to the adventure I shared with you and Rush. I will forever hold that time in my heart and consider you friends for a lifetime.

I shed tears of joy, and she will always remain a close family friend. Matt and Chuck had been so impressed with Sawyer that they'd gotten a puppy of their own from Tina about three months ago. It was a boy and they named him Holden. He was having fun revisiting his birthplace and playing with some of the other dogs. He tried playing with Rush, but he was all about hanging with me at the moment.

It was fun catching up, but after a few hours I was feeling anxious to get home with my wife and Rush. It was still a three hour drive. As we wrapped things up and headed to the jeep, Tina grabbed my arm. "Wait," she said. "I have a surprise for you."

I laughed. "I'm not sure I can handle any more surprises."

"Oh, you'll handle this one," my wife said.

I looked at her amused expression as Tina disappeared behind the house. A few minutes later she came back holding a puppy. "Meet your new family member. We all named him Finn."

I looked at all present and realized they had been in on this the whole time. Well, except for Rush I think. He had the same shocked look on his face I had.

Rush

What new fresh hell is this? I think I'd prefer the bear over a brother!

The End

ACKNOWLEDGEMENT

I'd like to thank the following people:

My friends Matt, Chuck, and Tina for letting me use their names and certain details of their life.

My editor, Kristine Laco, for her steadfast slaying of overused adverbs on my part. This book is much better for her guidance. Her services are available at www.kristinelaco.com.

Most of all, my wife, Michelle. She shares me enough with the real trails, and her support dealing with the mundane things while I was off writing in my fantasy world is what made this all possible.

No thanks, but I guess I'll kind of acknowledge the real life Ranger Dick too. In reality, his actions were in no way as despicable as portrayed in this book, but he's still a dick. I don't know his real name, but he knows who he is.

ABOUT THE AUTHOR

Lee Lovelace

The author is a fifty something dude who hasn't quite grown up. As long as he can remember, he wanted to be a writer but kept putting it off until he finally managed to get his act together.

A number of years ago he fell in love with The Appalachian Trail and all things hiking related. He lives a full-time RV life with his wife, Michelle, and two golden retrievers, Sawyer, and Finn. He is constantly traveling with his family while pretending to do a remote "real" job so he can take their money while also writing.

REVIEW

If you liked this book (or even if you didn't) please leave a review on Amazon. Reviews are often the only way self-publishing authors can get the word out about their work. So if you do, I'll love you long time. Probably not in the way that sounded, but I'll love you all the same.

Made in the USA
Columbia, SC
27 September 2023